喚醒你的英文語感!

Get a Feel for English !

喚醒你的英文語感！

Get a Feel for English!

To master a language is to repeat, refine, and remember.

Phrase Power
英文短語的力量

作者 / 劉怡均
閱讀文章撰寫 / Andrew E. Bennett

主題語境輸入　關鍵詞組擴充　反覆內化應用

培養閱讀素養　訓練雙語轉換　提升考場說寫力
與批判思維　與記憶強化　鍛鍊邏輯表達

貝塔│語測　高點│美語系列
檢測學習平台

CONTENTS

導讀 __ 4

● **PART 1**　環境與永續發展

TOPIC 1 Environmental Restoration 環境復育 __ 13

TOPIC 2 The Global Water Crisis 全球水資源危機 __ 25

TOPIC 3 China's Dust Storm Crisis 沙塵暴挑戰 __ 37

TOPIC 4 Carbon Emissions 碳排放 __ 49

● **PART 2**　文化現象與變遷

TOPIC 5 Gossip Culture 八卦文化 __ 61

TOPIC 6 Culture Without Borders 世界地球村 __ 71

TOPIC 7 Aging Society 高齡社會 __ 81

TOPIC 8 Welcome to the Age of Avatars 虛擬分身時代來臨 __ 91

TOPIC 9 How English Evolved 英語的演變 __ 101

PART 3　藝術、風格與文化

TOPIC 10 Sotheby's 蘇富比 ___ 113

TOPIC 11 Go Retro 復古風 ___ 123

TOPIC 12 Lost Arts 失落的藝術 ___ 135

PART 4　城市與旅遊

TOPIC 13 Adventure Tourism 冒險旅遊 ___ 149

TOPIC 14 New York 紐約 ___ 159

TOPIC 15 London 倫敦 ___ 169

PART 5　科普與未來趨勢

TOPIC 16 Yoga 瑜伽 ___ 181

TOPIC 17 Forensic Science 鑑識科學 ___ 191

TOPIC 18 Franchising 加盟商機 ___ 201

TOPIC 19 Living in Space 太空生活 ___ 211

TOPIC 20 The Promise and Controversy of Stem Cells
　　　　　幹細胞的潛力與爭議 ___ 221

導讀

　　大家都知道，字彙是英語學習的基礎，但問題在於──如何才能真正記住並正確使用這些字彙？如果有一種方法，可以讓你一看到字彙就秒記住，並且能夠運用自如，不管是需要開口說或是動筆寫，無論何時何地，你都能自然地使用道地英語來表達，那該有多好？你將不再面臨那種說／寫到一半就卡卡的困境，更不會說／寫出中式英文，是不是太美妙了！

　　首先我們要破除一個迷思──「單字不用背」這件事情！

這個 slogan 幾乎無處不在，但它並不像字面上看起來那麼簡單。打著「單字不用背」的口號並不是告訴你，學習英語詞彙輕而易舉，不需要特別做什麼事情，詞彙就會自動輸入你的大腦。若你這樣想，那你是否也相信世界上有「記憶吐司」這種好東西呢？

　　「單字不用背」這個口號背後有一件非常重要的事情：單字不是不用背，是你背不起啊！

如果把「背」跟「死記硬背」畫上等號，那麼背單字的任務會變得像是要你把進小巨蛋看演唱會的上萬人名字背起來一樣可怕，這根本是不可能的任務吧！換句話說，「單字不用背」並不是一條捷徑的保證，它是一個提醒！光靠死記硬背行不通，那我們要怎麼辦？

　　除非，有方法。

例如：要是你將看演唱會的茫茫人海按姓氏分類，然後再把每一類用更多不同的方式仔細區分，比如說，還可以分出鮭魚的一類、有忠孝節義的一類等等。如此便能越分越小，小到你可以熟悉掌握的程度。這樣一比喻，大家馬上能夠聯想到「字根字首」對吧！但是，請先不要高興得太早，想要掌握英文單字，不是只要你知道某個字的字根字首之後，就心領神「會」了。就好像那場演唱會裡，在鮭魚分類底下的那五十個人，你雖然知道他們都跟鮭魚有關係，但他們就不是鮭魚啊！他們可能是「鮭魚刺身」、「鮭魚手捲」、「鮭魚茶泡飯」、「鮭魚卵」，這些詞組雖然都屬於「鮭魚」這個分類條目，但是他們都有「各自獨立的人生」。

如果你只是爲了短期應付考試，只求能在考試中提高猜中的機率就好，你或許可以不用在乎這些詞彙「各自的人生」，但是英語學習對你來說，就會淪落成這樣的窘境，明明國高中學／背了很多，可是畢業之後在眞實生活裡、職場上，聽也聽不是太懂、讀也讀不太明白、想說但是說不出來、想寫直接去問 AI……

> **「單字們各自獨立的人生」是什麼？**
>
> 想想看，如果它是動詞，那是及物還是不及物（跟用法有關）？如果是形容詞，那它又偏好去依附在哪些名詞身邊（跟搭配詞有關）？又或者，從字根字首的拆解來看是一個意思，但是其實引申含義又是另外一個意思，而現代英語常用的就是該字的引申義……換言之，字根字首只是幫助你分類茫茫字海的一個很好的開端，而後面要真正內化吸收所有字彙，你還有很多事情要做呢！

如果你希望學習英語不再止步於此，那麼讓我們來談談有效且實用的學習方法吧！

學習字彙的關鍵在於「反覆」

沒有反覆，沒有記住；沒有反覆，沒有深度；沒有反覆，沒有進步。

單字就像一個名字，像一個經文符號，要將這種符號烙印在腦海裡，比較像拓印石碑，而不是像「影印機」一樣可以馬上完成。拓印需要反覆的輕敲、細緻的打磨，需要時間和耐心，學習英語也是如此。

單字學習的基本功就是跟每個詞彙一次、又一次、再一次的「確認過眼神」！就如同我們國小學習寫國字，每個字都要寫十遍，這樣反覆練習能幫助你牢記該生字。可是當我們學習第二外語時，這個「反覆」過程會稍微複雜一些——並不是單純地把 appetite（食慾）寫十遍而已，這個做法是沒有效果的。以下用 appetite 為例，說明這個「反覆」的學習旅程，並且導讀本書的使用方式。如果能將這個略嫌複雜的學習方式確實執行，你將可以預見自己的雙語人生要開始走花路了！

1. 學習詞彙時，要保留上下文
把單字放入完整語境中，整串詞組一起打包帶走。

比如說你在閱讀文章中看到這一句：

Celebrity gossip is everywhere because we have such a huge **appetite** for it.
名人八卦無處不在，因為我們對它有著強烈的興趣。

假設你要學習 appetite 這個字，千萬不要讓單字「孤身一人」，而是要把它「左鄰右舍」的詞彙都一起帶走，所以你抄寫下來的應該是 **We have such a huge appetite for it.**（我們對×××有強烈的興趣）。如此一來，你學到的是單字的語境、用法以及搭配詞，這樣學習單字不僅容易記住，日後也能更靈活地運用它。

2. 開始「反覆」的旅程
將你學到的詞組反覆朗讀、抄寫並照樣造句，
當你反覆使用這些詞彙，它們會逐漸轉化為長期記憶。

我們延續上面 appetite 這個例子來說明：

文章當中原句反覆

We **have such a huge <u>appetite</u> for** celebrity gossip.〔讀或寫第一次〕
We **have such a huge <u>appetite</u> for** celebrity gossip.〔讀或寫第二次〕
……
We **have such a huge <u>appetite</u> for** celebrity gossip.〔讀或寫第 N 次〕

照樣造句練習

His appetite for adventure led him to travel the world.
他對冒險的渴望讓他踏遍世界。
She has an insatiable appetite for learning new things.
她對學習新事物有強烈的渴望，怎麼學都不夠。

3. 在腦中建立雙語友好橋樑
學會將單字與語境互相對應，而非僵硬的直譯。

看看以下英文例句，appetite 這個字在這裡是什麼意思呢？

Celebrity gossip is everywhere because **we have such a huge <u>appetite</u> for it**.

appetite 有 the feeling that you want to eat food，也有 the feeling of wanting or needing something 的意思，也可以表示 taste or preference。而在這個例句裡，appetite 不是指對食物的渴望（食慾），而是對於事物的強烈興趣或偏好。

從上述的例子可以看出來，比較理想的認識詞彙方法是，先用英文來解釋英文單字（請花一點時間留意英英字典詞條定義解釋的文字），參考英文例句，並用「相應」的中文詞彙來描述其含義，然後將這兩大塊豐富的詞彙搭配在一起來回反覆熟記。

4. 把母語詞彙換句話說

例如：She **lost her appetite** due to stress.
　　　她因為壓力很大，沒什麼食慾。

除了「沒什麼食慾」這個說法之外，還有哪些更口語、或是更文雅的說法呢？比如說，都沒什麼胃口、吃不下東西、食慾不振、食不知味……。

> **❝ 小叮嚀 ❞**
>
> 請記得，這個步驟「不是逐字翻譯」，而是要使用平易近人、且能貼近你生活的自然口語用字！因此，你會有一種以上的相應描述。

這樣的例子旨在告訴大家，雙語之間並非單純「一個蘿蔔一個坑」的唯一對應關係，兩種語言的文化背景與語法結構差異相當大。若想在雙語之間流暢轉換，就必須擺脫「appetite＝食慾」這種僵化的學習方式。要能實現流暢的雙語切換，關鍵在於發揮中文母語的彈性。在說英文時，若你能在母語中找到多種換句話說的方式，那麼你的英文表達自然也能對應出合適且道地的詞語。

5. 重複有三種層次

　　第一層重複是透過抄寫原句和造句練習來進行。這是學習的初步階段，幫助你把新學的詞彙和結構牢牢記住。

　　若你能透過閱聽方式持續接觸英語環境，你就會有源源不絕的機會進入第二層重複，當你閱讀其他文章或觀看電影、電視劇時，假設又出現類似 have a big appetite for 的表達，你的記憶會被再次強化。這也是為什麼讓自己持續接觸英語環境對於學習這個語言至關重要，鼓勵自己定時定量的閱讀英語素材，就是提供自己不間斷的複習機會，最終這些用字語法會深深烙印在你的腦海中，想忘也忘不掉。

第三層重複出現在你實際使用英語的過程中，無論是口語表達還是寫作，當你想說「胃口大開」或是「我超愛……的東西」，甚至是「我對……完全沒有抵抗力」時，你會想起 have a big appetite for，這樣的「輸出」練習不僅能加深對這個詞組的記憶，還有助於將聽、說、讀、寫四項能力相互融合，讓你的語言運用更加靈活自如。

這本書，就是上述這個「反覆」學習旅程的濃縮精華。通過本書，你將學會如何將這些有效的方法融入日常生活繼續實踐，畢竟這趟旅程沒有終點。書中每個單元都包括實用的詞彙和例句練習，讓你不僅能學到單字，還能學會如何在真實語境中運用它們。只要你持續反覆學習，你的英語能力一定會穩步提升。

以 Gossip Culture 這個單元為例，閱讀文章中有八組詞組被以粗體字醒目標示。練習 A 將針對這八組詞組進行應用練習，例句會是與 Gossip Culture 主題相關的中文短句，並且在相應的中文詞彙上做醒目標示（如下面例子）。

4 have such a huge appetite for it
人們對八卦有著強烈的渴望，總是很難抵擋釣魚式標題的誘惑。

有了以上醒目提示的加持，請試著將整句中文翻譯成英文。放輕鬆，這不是嚴格的翻譯考試，而是為了讓你能夠在日後活用這些英語詞彙進行反覆學習。練習 A 的目的是幫助你熟悉這些詞組，對於將中文語句用英文來表達，目標是先求有（能說就好），再求好（參考練習 B 中的翻譯建議）。

練習 B 會提供練習 A 的英文句子參考說法。要注意的是，這些中英例句之間沒有所謂的「中央標準答案」，這並不是本書的目的！如果你在看了例句之後，聯想到其他的表達方式，或者自己已經可以換句話說，這都是很好的練習。此外，在練習 B 裡，例句的開頭留有一個空白（如下面例子），這個設計是為了讓你去回想一下，have such a huge appetite for gossip 在中文裡能夠有哪些類似的表達方式，能夠順利反應出這些相似卻有些微差異的說法，對日後雙語切換的彈性有很大的幫助。

4 (　　　　　　　)
People have such a huge appetite for gossip that they can't resist clickbait headlines.

　　練習 C 和練習 D 的設計與前兩個練習類似，都是先提供中文再搭配英文的練習，唯一不同的是，這些例句的適用範圍更廣，涵蓋日常生活中的各種情境。換句話說，這些練習示範了如何在不同語境中使用這些詞組，從而幫助你掌握更靈活多變的語言表達。

　　每一單元的最後還有〈關鍵短語 1 ＋ 1 大於 2〉的「延伸學習」。除了原本從閱讀文章中挑選出來的詞組之外，還增加了類似的實用表達，例如 have a huge appetite for 可以和 can't get enough of（超愛、怎麼都不會膩）或 endlessly scrolling through（滑手機滑個不停）等詞組一起學習，這樣你就能在生活對話情境中舉一反三的活用相關語彙。

　　相信你讀到這裡，已經開始理解語言學習的本質，它是一個不斷吸收反饋並進行實踐的過程。只要不斷重複，你就會記住。祝福翻開本書的你，突破自我，學而能有所用，並在學習這條路上永不止步，持續探索，創造屬於自己的精彩人生。

Nana 劉怡均

Environment & Sustainability
環境與永續發展

PART 1

TOPIC 1

Environmental Restoration:
Healing the Planet for Future Generations

環境復育：為了未來世代守護地球

沙漠化

全球暖化

森林正快速消失
能再生嗎？

Reading

MP3 01

閱讀以下文章，粗體字部分是本文的關鍵短語，先想想它們的意思及用法，再跟著引導進行更多字彙擴充練習！

The world's forests are disappearing. **For a number of reasons**, that's cause for alarm. Governments, NGOs (non-governmental organizations), and private individuals **are taking steps to reverse this trend**. Through small- and large-scale reforestation activities, **they're nursing forests back to life**.

Some 13 million hectares of forest are cut down every year. In some cases, timber and mining companies are to blame. At other times, forests are cleared to **make room for** new farms, or the cleared land is used to raise livestock.

The yearly loss has been severe in some parts of the world. From 2000 to 2010, 3.4 million hectares were lost every year in South America and Africa. In Vietnam, 51 percent of the country's primary forests — meaning forests never touched by human activity — vanished from 2000 to 2005.

In many places, including Vietnam, replanting efforts **are under way** to restore damaged or destroyed forests. **The first step is to** identify the species of trees that are native to the area. Ideally, a variety of species are planted. That improves an area's biodiversity. Over the next two years, the newly planted seedlings are monitored to make sure they grow healthily.

Reforestation efforts have had **mixed results**. More than 7 million hectares of forest are replanted annually. In Costa Rica, for example, the Cloudbridge River Project is restoring an important section of forest. Some countries, unfortunately, have been less successful in their efforts. Illegal tree harvesting and livestock over-grazing are among the problems they face.

Despite such setbacks, reforestation efforts are spreading. More countries are **becoming aware of** the benefits of having healthy forests. They improve the soil, stop the spread of deserts, and protect the ground water. Forests also help in the fight against global warming by removing carbon gases from the air. Finally, healthy forests make the land more beautiful **for future generations**.

翻譯

全球的森林正在消失，其背後牽連的原因廣泛，這是一個值得關注的問題。為了扭轉這一局勢，各國政府、非政府組織 (NGOs) 以及個人都在積極行動，希望透過大小規模的造林計畫，讓森林可以重新恢復生機。

每年約有 1,300 萬公頃的森林被砍伐，背後的原因不盡相同。有些是因為伐木和採礦產業的開發；有些則是為了開墾農地或放牧牲畜，而清除大面積森林。

在某些地區，森林消失的速度相當驚人。從 2000 年到 2010 年，南美洲和非洲每年流失 340 萬公頃的森林。在越南，原始森林（即從未經人類開發或影響的森林）更是在 2000 到 2005 年間減少了 51%。

所幸，許多國家正展開森林復育計畫，包括越南在內，許多受破壞的森林地區都開始進行重新植樹的行動。第一步是確認當地的原生樹種，並儘量種植多種不同的樹木，以提升生物多樣性。新種植的樹苗會在接下來的兩年內受到密切監測，以確保它們能夠健康成長。

然而，森林復育的成果好壞參半。全球每年約有 700 萬公頃的森林被復育，例如哥斯大黎加的 Cloudbridge River Project 正在努力恢復一片重要的林地。但並非所有國家的造林計畫都順利推動，像是非法砍伐和牲畜過度放牧等問題，對某些國家來說仍是有待突破的考驗。

儘管如此，森林復育的行動仍在持續拓展。越來越多國家開始意識到健康森林可以帶來的種種好處：它們能夠改善土壤品質、阻止沙漠化、保護地下水資源，甚至還能透過吸收二氧化碳來降低大氣中的碳含量，幫助減緩全球暖化。此外，茂密的森林還能讓環境變得更美麗，為後代子孫留下更好的生活空間。

PLUS! 主題實用詞彙精選

- [ ] cause for alarm 令人憂心 / 警惕
- [ ] be to blame 是……的原因
- [ ] primary forests 原始森林
- [ ] illegal tree harvesting 非法砍伐
- [ ] over-grazing 過度放牧
- [ ] ground water 地下水

Environmental Restoration

練習 A：用英文表達

Phrase in Action

用以下關鍵短語作為句子重點提示，試著用英文表達每一句話。不一定只有一種說法！

1　take steps to
這座城市正在採取行動來改善空氣品質。

2　make room for
我們需要在城市裡騰出更多空間給綠地。

3　back to life
森林能夠再生嗎？答案是肯定的，現在有些計畫正在幫助森林恢復原貌。

4　under way
推廣再生能源的計畫正在進行中。

5　The first step is to
第一步是減少一次性塑膠產品，但更重要的是，我們必須讓大眾明白這件事的迫切性。

> 1～5 這些短語都與行動、計畫、變化有關，通常用來描述事情的進展或措施。

6　for future generations
永續能源是未來世代擁有更好環境的關鍵。

7　for a number of reasons
因為種種原因，我們應該更常搭乘大眾運輸。

> 6～10 的短語多用於解釋原因、結果、影響或情境，通常是在補充說明或提供背景資訊。

8　despite such setbacks
很多政府因為經濟考量猶豫不決，不太願意推行嚴格的環保政策。儘管如此，還是有很多人一直在努力，為了讓環境變得更好。

9　mixed results
這座城市從去年開始禁用塑膠吸管，但效果好壞參半。有些店換成了紙吸管，但有些乾脆改用塑膠杯蓋。

10　becoming aware of
越來越多人開始意識到回收的重要性。

16

Environmental Restoration

MP3 02

練習 B：記憶挑戰 Phrase Recall!

以下是練習A各句子的參考英文說法，但關鍵短語不見了！你還記得它的中文怎麼說嗎？
*Reference Only – Not the Only Way!

1 (　　正在採取行動　　)
The city is **taking steps to** improve air quality.

2 (　　　　　　　　)
We need to **make room for** more green spaces in the city.

3 (　　　　　　　　)
Is it possible to bring a forest **back to life**? The answer is yes—some projects are helping forests reclaim their old territories.

4 (　　　　　　　　)
Projects **are under way** to promote renewable energy.

5 (　　　　　　　　)
The first step is to reduce single-use plastic products, but more importantly, we need to raise awareness about the urgency of this issue.

6 (　　　　　　　　)
Sustainable energy is the key to a better world **for future generations**.

7 (　　　　　　　　)
For a number of reasons, we should switch to public transportation more often.

8 (　　　　　　　　)
Many governments are reluctant to implement strict environmental policies due to economic concerns. **Despite such setbacks**, people keep fighting for environmental protection.

9 (　　　　　　　　)
The city banned plastic straws last year, and so far, **there have been mixed results**. Some businesses switched to paper straws, but others just went back to plastic lids.

10 (　　　　　　　　)
More people are **becoming aware of** the importance of recycling.

TOPIC ❶ 環境復育

Let's Chat!

練習 C：靈活應用 Phrase Remix!
同樣的短語，放進生活其他情境中應用看看！
你也可以試著造自己的句子！

1　take steps to
我的室友正在按照計畫逐步努力，想要獲得綠卡。

2　make room for
放下負面情緒，心才能騰出空間去成長。

3　back to life
度假讓我整個人都活了過來——陽光、美食，還有不看工作信箱，這樣就夠了。

4　under way
公司正在進行調整，包括彈性工時和遠距工作選擇，以改善員工的工作與生活平衡。

5　The first step is to
遇到複雜的問題，急著找速成解法通常沒用。第一步應該是先搞清楚問題本身，而不是急著下定論。

6　for future generations
做資源回收不只是為了現在，也是為了我們的下一代。

7　for a number of reasons
因為種種原因，我決定與某些人保持距離。

8　despite such setbacks
她試鏡一次又一次被刷掉，有時候連房租都繳不出來。儘管如此，她還是不願放棄自己的夢想。

9　mixed results
線上學習的效果不一。有些學生在家會比較專心，有些學生反而容易分心。

10　becoming aware of
越來越多人開始意識到心理健康真的很重要。

Let's Chat!

MP3 03

練習 D：記憶挑戰 Phrase Recall!

以下是練習 C 各句子的參考英文說法，但關鍵短語不見了，而且還變長了！試著用你的話來描述這些被標示的語言段！

Reference Only – Not the Only Way!

1 （ 著手申請綠卡的步驟 ）
My roommate is taking steps to obtain her green card.

2 （   ）
Letting go of negativity makes room for self-growth.

3 （   ）
A good vacation brings me back to life—some sunshine, good food, and no emails. That's all I need.

4 （   ）
Major changes are under way to improve work-life balance, including flexible work hours and remote work options.

5 （   ）
Oversimplifying complex issues and rushing to quick fixes won't help. The first step should be identifying the problem rather than jumping to conclusions.

6 （   ）
Recycling isn't just for now—it's for future generations.

7 （   ）
For a number of reasons, I decided to distance myself from certain people.

8 （   ）
She failed her auditions over and over again, sometimes she couldn't even pay her rent. Despite such setbacks, she never gave up on her dreams.

9 （   ）
Online learning has had mixed results. Some students find it easier to stay focused at home, while others get distracted.

10 （   ）
People are becoming far more aware of the importance of mental health.

TOPIC ❶ 環境復育   19

Expand! （關鍵短語1 + 1 > 2 !!）   MP3 04

看看本單元學過的關鍵短語，還可以延伸出哪些相關說法呢？繼續擴充你的口說及寫作素材吧！

1
- **for future generations** 為了未來世代
- **leave behind a legacy** 傳承、留下深遠影響
- **pass something down** 傳承
- **think long-term** 長遠思考

You want to **leave a legacy**. You need to **think long-term** and make responsible choices.
眼光放長遠，做出負責任的選擇，為未來世代留下寶貴的資產。

Through storytelling, we can **pass down wisdom and values** to future generations.
透過說故事的方式，我們可以將智慧與價值信念傳承給後代。

2
- **for a number of reasons** 因為各種原因
- **for multiple reasons** 因為多種原因
- **for all sorts of reasons** 因為各種原因
- **for obvious reasons** 顯而易見

I started taking the bus **for multiple reasons**. It's cheaper, less stressful, and better for the environment.
我開始搭公車，原因很多，比較省錢、不那麼累，對環境也比較友善。

She moved out of the city **for all sorts of reasons**—the noise, living costs, and the hectic pace of life.
她搬離城市，原因有很多──太吵、太貴，還有快速的生活步調。

A: So, what happened at the meeting last night?
B: I can't say much right now, **for obvious reasons**.
A: Wait... the big boss is stepping down? For real?!
B: Let's just say... you'll find out soon enough.

A：昨晚的會議到底發生了什麼？
B：我不能透露細節，至於為什麼不能透露，不用我說你也知道吧。
A：等等……老闆要辭職？真的假的？！
B：只能說……你很快就會知道了。

3
take steps to 正在採取行動
make an effort to 努力去做（某事）
work toward 朝著……努力
make progress in 在……方面有所進展

We are **taking steps to** improve sustainability by **making an effort to** reduce waste, **working toward** a greener future, and **making progress in** developing eco-friendly alternatives.
我們正在採取行動促進永續發展，努力減少浪費，朝著更環保的未來邁進，並在開發環保替代方案方面有所進展。

4
back to life 恢復生機
on the verge of 瀕臨
rise from the ashes 浴火重生

The historic market was **on the verge of being forgotten**, but after a massive renovation, it **has come back to life**. Now, it has truly **risen from the ashes**, attracting visitors from all over the world.
這個歷史悠久的市場本來已經漸漸被人們遺忘，經過大規模維護整理之後，又重新恢復生機。如今，它浴火重生，吸引了來自世界各地的遊客。

5
make room for 騰出空間
clear space for 清出空間給
prioritize 優先考慮

We need to **make room for new ideas and clear space for creativity**, which means we have to **prioritize what truly matters**.
我們要有空間才能接收新的想法，才能讓創意發揮，說白了，就是得搞清楚哪些事才是對我們真正重要的事情。

TOPIC **1** 環境復育　21

6
be under way 正在進行中
in progress 正在進行
on track 在正確的軌道上

Big changes **are under way to** improve the city, and several new projects **are in progress**. Everything is **on track**.
城市正在進行重大改革，許多新專案也在進行中，一切都在按計畫進行。

7
The first step is to 第一步是⋯⋯
start with 從⋯⋯開始

The first step is to try to relax and clear your mind. **Start with** a deep breath and allow yourself to be fully present.
第一步是試著放鬆並整理思緒。從深呼吸開始，讓自己完全專注在當下。

8
mixed results 好壞參半
hit or miss 要碰運氣，有時好，有時壞
some ups and downs 有好有壞

Trying a new diet can **have mixed results**—it's pretty **hit or miss**. There will be **some ups and downs**, so it's important to find what works best for you.
嘗試新飲食方式可能好壞參半，效果不一定。過程中也難免感覺有好有壞，所以找到適合自己的方式很重要。

9
Despite such setbacks 儘管遭遇挫折
bounce back from 從⋯⋯中恢復
in the face of challenges 面對挑戰

Despite such setbacks, she managed to **bounce back from** failure and stay strong **in the face of challenges**.
儘管遇到那些打擊，她並沒有倒下，她熬了過來而且面對挑戰依舊不退縮。

become aware of 開始意識到
⑩ wake up to 驚覺
gain a better understanding of 更清楚了解

I used to scroll through social media for hours. But one night, I realized it was 3 AM and I had wasted the entire evening. That was the moment I **woke up to** how much time I was throwing away every day.
我以前常常一滑臉書就滑很久。有一天，我發現怎麼已經凌晨三點了，而我整個晚上什麼事情都沒有做。就是那一刻，我突然驚覺，原來我每天浪費了那麼多時間在社群媒體上面。

After the incident, more people **gained a better understanding of** what climate change really means. It's no longer some far-off problem; it is happening now.
這次事件之後，越來越多人更清楚地了解氣候變遷的真正意義──這不是一個距離我們還很遙遠的問題，而是此刻在發生的現實。

Notes

TOPIC 2

The Global Water Crisis
全球水資源危機

水。

過度使用

60％的水被浪費了

水位急劇下降

3.5億人的

危機由

健康

污染

Reading

MP3 05

閱讀以下文章，粗體字部分是本文的關鍵短語，先想想它們的意思及用法，再跟著引導進行更多字彙擴充練習！

Water is our most important natural resource. Yet though water covers most of the Earth, only 2.5% of it is salt-free. **Demand for fresh water has risen sharply** in the last 50 years, and **it is still going up**. That's already causing serious problems. Finding the right solutions may **be one of the biggest challenges of our time**.

There are several reasons behind the growing crisis. The first is waste. About 70% of our fresh water is used to grow crops. It takes 1,000 tons of water to grow just one ton of wheat. Unfortunately, around 60% of that water is wasted. Better irrigation methods **would help the situation**.

Pollution is another big problem. Many of the world's great rivers, such as the Ganges in India, are badly polluted. Yet 350 million people **rely on** the Ganges. Their health **is affected by** the health of the river. Steps are being taken to clean up some waterways, but it is expensive and **can take years**.

Overuse also **puts pressure on** water supplies. In the USA, 95% of the country's fresh water comes from underground sources. With so much water being used to grow crops and raise livestock, water levels are dropping rapidly. **Once used, those supplies are gone forever**, since they are not refilled by rainwater. The key there is to lower demand.

In many places around the world, **people already live in crisis**. More than one billion people have no access to clean water. That leads to millions of deaths every year, including thousands of children dying every day in Africa. By 2025, as many as 25 African countries may face severe water shortages. The situation could even lead to wars over water rights.

The fresh water crisis is not limited to poor regions. Indeed, rich and poor countries from Asia to Europe to North America are facing shortages. It's a growing problem **that could soon affect us all**.

翻譯

水是我們最重要的自然資源。然而，儘管水覆蓋了地球的大部分，但只有 2.5% 的水是淡水。過去 50 年來，對淡水的需求急劇上升，並且仍在持續增長。這已經造成了嚴重的問題。找到合適的解決方案可能是我們這個時代最大的挑戰之一。

這場日益嚴重的危機背後有幾個原因。首先是浪費。大約 70% 的淡水用於灌溉農作物。僅僅種植一噸小麥就需要 1,000 噸水。不幸的是，大約 60% 的水被浪費了。更好的灌溉方法將有助於改善這個情況。

污染是另一大問題。許多世界著名的大河流都受到嚴重污染，如印度的恆河。然而，有 3.5 億人依賴恆河，他們的健康直接受河流健康的影響。雖然已有採取措施來清理一些水道，但這些需花費大量的金錢，並且需要相當長的時間。

過度使用也是對水資源的巨大壓力。在美國，95% 的淡水來自地下水源。由於大量水被用來種植農作物和飼養牲畜，水位急遽下降。一旦用完，這些水資源將永遠消失，因為它們無法通過降水補充。關鍵在於要降低需求。

在世界上許多地方，人們已經生活在危機當中。超過十億人無法獲得乾淨的水源，這導致每年數百萬人死亡，其中非洲每天有數千名兒童死亡。到 2025 年，可能有多達 25 個非洲國家將面臨嚴重的水資源短缺。這種情況甚至可能引發爭奪水資源的戰爭。

淡水危機不僅限於貧困地區。事實上，從亞洲到歐洲再到北美的富裕或貧窮國家，都面臨著水資源短缺。這是一個日益嚴重的問題，可能很快會影響到我們所有人。

PLUS! 主題實用詞彙精選

- ☐ fresh water 淡水
- ☐ growing crisis 日益加劇的危機
- ☐ irrigation method 灌溉方式
- ☐ water supply 供水
- ☐ have no access to 無法取得（資源）
- ☐ severe water shortage 嚴重水資源短缺

The Global Water Crisis

練習 A：用英文表達

Phrase in Action

用以下關鍵短語作為句子重點提示，試著用英文表達每一句話。不一定只有一種說法！

1 Demand for... has risen sharply, and it's still going up.
淡水需求急劇上升，並且仍在持續增加，而全球水資源卻在減少。

2 be one of the biggest challenges of our time
解決水資源危機是當今人類面臨最艱難的挑戰之一。

3 would help the situation
在家節約用水，其實比我們想像的更有助益。

4 can take years
修復一條受污染的河川需要很長時間，但人類一時的疏忽卻能在短時間內讓它受到嚴重破壞。

5 rely on... is affected by
城市生活仰賴穩定的水資源供應，但是穩定的未來取決於我們今天如何用水。

> 1～5：描述當前局勢與挑戰，這些短語可以用來強調目前的情況、需求和問題背景，並為討論提供清晰的基礎。

6 puts pressure on
氣候變遷對水資源造成壓力，使乾旱變得更加嚴重。

7 Once overused, ... gone forever
一旦被過度使用，深層地下水幾乎無法恢復。

8 people already live in crisis
有些地區的人早就生活在水資源危機中，連安全飲水都很難取得。

9 that could soon affect us all
如果現在不行動，全球缺水問題很快就會影響到我們每一個人。

> 6～9：強調「行為後果與未來風險」
> 這些短語描述「如果當前情況持續下去，將會出現的後果或風險」，強調行為對未來的影響。

The Global Water Crisis

MP3 06

練習 B：記憶挑戰 Phrase Recall!

以下是練習A各句子的參考英文說法，但關鍵短語不見了！你還記得它的中文怎麼說嗎？

Reference Only - Not the Only Way!

1（對……需求大增，而且還在持續上升中）
Demand for fresh water has risen sharply, and it's still going up, while the global water supply is shrinking.

2（   ）
Solving the water crisis is one of the toughest challenges of our time facing humanity today.

3（   ）
Reducing water waste at home would help the situation more than we realize.

4（   ）
Restoring a polluted river can take years—but careless actions can ruin it far more quickly.

5（   ）
Modern cities rely on steady water supplies, but the future is affected by how wisely we use water today.

6（   ）
Climate change puts pressure on water resources, causing more intense droughts.

7（   ）
Once overused, deep groundwater is nearly gone forever.

8（   ）
In some regions, people already live in crisis, struggling to find safe drinking water.

9（   ）
If we don't act now, the global water shortage could soon affect us all.

TOPIC ❷ 全球水資源危機

Let's Chat!

練習 C：靈活應用 Phrase Remix!
同樣的短語，放進生活其他情境中應用看看！
你也可以試著造自己的句子！

1 Demand for... has risen sharply, and it's still going up.
對房屋的需求大增，且仍在持續增加中。

2 be one of the biggest challenges of our time
心理健康問題已經成為我們這個時代最大的挑戰之一。

3 would help the situation
多一點耐心和理解，會讓情況好很多。

4 can take years
建立深厚的友誼可能需要數年，但破壞它卻只要一瞬間。

5 rely on... is affected by
父母仰賴學校來教育孩子，但孩子的成長受到許多因素的影響，比如遺傳、營養，以及家庭與社交生活。

6 puts pressure on
食品價格不斷上漲，讓預算吃緊的家庭承受更大壓力。

7 Once, ... gone forever.
信任一旦被打破，就永遠無法挽回。

8 people already live in crisis
許多年長者已經生活在困境中，努力對抗孤獨與不足的支援。

9 that could soon affect us all
人工智慧的快速崛起正在改變各行各業，這可能很快影響到我們所有人。

Let's Chat!

MP3 07

練習 D：記憶挑戰 Phrase Recall!

以下是練習 C 各句子的參考英文說法，但關鍵短語不見了，而且還變長了！試著用你的話來描述這些被標示的語言段！

Reference Only – Not the Only Way!

1 (　　　　　　　　　　　)
Demand for housing has risen sharply, and it's still going up.

2 (　　　　　　　　　　　　　　　)
Mental health struggles have become one of the biggest challenges of our time.

3 (　　　　　　　　)
A little more patience and understanding would help the situation.

4 (　　　　　　　　)
Building a strong friendship can take years, but breaking it only takes a moment.

5 (　　　　　　　　　　　　　　)
Parents rely on schools to educate their children, but a child's growth is affected by many factors, such as genetics, nutrition, and family and social life.

6 (　　　　　　　　　)
Rising food prices put pressure on families with tight budgets.

7 (　　　　　　　　)
Once broken, trust is gone forever.

8 (　　　　　　　　　)
Many elderly people already live in crisis, struggling with loneliness and a lack of support.

9 (　　　　　　　　)
The rapid rise of artificial intelligence is reshaping industries and could soon affect us all.

TOPIC ❷ 全球水資源危機

Expand! （關鍵短語 1 + 1 > 2 !!）

MP3 08

看看本單元學過的關鍵短語，還可以延伸出哪些相關說法呢？繼續擴充你的口說及寫作素材吧！

1
Demand for... has risen sharply, and it's still going up.
對⋯⋯的需求大增，且仍在上升

People are looking for... more than ever, and it's only increasing.
人們對⋯⋯的需求比以往更高，且還在增加

More and more people want..., and the demand keeps growing.
越來越多人想要⋯⋯，需求不斷增長

There's never been a greater need for..., and it's still rising.
對⋯⋯的需求前所未有地高，而且還在上升

Demand for therapy services has risen sharply, and it's still going up. Lockdowns and financial struggles have taken an emotional toll on individuals. At the same time, mental health is no longer seen as a taboo. Schools, workplaces, and even social media platforms are openly discussing that it's okay to be not okay. **That's why there has never been a greater need for accessible mental health support.**

對心理諮商的需求大增，且仍在上升。在經歷封城以及隨之而來的經濟壓力後，越來越多人開始尋求幫助。而且現在，心理健康不再是禁忌話題了。學校、工作場所，甚至社群媒體都能公開討論身心問題。所以，現在對心理健康資源的需求比以往任何時候都更為迫切。

2
Once overused, ... gone forever 一旦被過度消耗，就永遠消失了
there's no way to restore it immediately 無法馬上恢復
if we waste it, it's gone for good. 如果浪費了，它就永遠消失了

If we keep cutting down trees like this, **the forests will be gone for good. There's no way to bring them back overnight.**
如果我們繼續這樣砍樹，森林就真的永遠消失了。這可不是一夜之間能恢復的。

be one of the biggest challenges of our time
是我們這個時代最大的挑戰之一

Few issues are as pressing as...
很少有問題比……更緊迫

③ One of the toughest problems we face today is...
我們今天面臨的最大問題之一是……

It's hard to deny that... is one of the greatest challenges of our time
無可否認，……是我們這個時代最大的挑戰之一

Finding work-life balance **has become one of the biggest challenges of our time**. It can feel like "a mission impossible" when one tries to squeeze in "me time." The truth is, **one of the toughest problems we face today** is the expectation to always be available. Maybe we need to be practical here. It's unrealistic to feel obligated to make everyone around us happy. What do you think? **Is making yourself happy**—without sacrificing too much and still taking care of the ones you love—**one of the greatest challenges of our time**?

找到工作與生活的平衡已經成為我們這個時代最大的挑戰之一。當我們試圖在忙碌的生活中擠出一點「跟自己好好相處」的時間時，往往會覺得這根本是「不可能的任務」。其實，現在面臨的一個大問題就是我們總被期待要隨時待命。也許我們應該現實一點，要讓周圍每一個人都快樂，這實在是不切實際。你怎麼看呢？在不過多犧牲自己，還能照顧到所愛的人的情況下，讓自己快樂，會是我們這個時代最難以克服的挑戰之一嗎？

rely on... is affected by 依賴……，受……影響

④ We count on..., but... have a big impact on it.
我們依賴……，但經常受到……的影響

We **rely on good sleep**, **but** stress and late-night screen time **often mess it up**.
我們需要好的睡眠，但壓力和睡前滑手機這些事情常常讓我們更睡不好。

We **count on our immune system** to keep us healthy, but what we eat and how we live **have a big impact on it.**
我們仰賴免疫系統來維持健康，但飲食和生活習慣對它影響很大。

> **would help the situation** 有助於改善情況
> ❺ **One way to make things better is...** 讓情況變好的其中一個方法是……
> **If we could..., it would help a lot.** 如果我們能……，情況會改善很多

Talking openly about it **would really help the situation**. **One way to make things better is to** make therapy more affordable. Also, **if we could break the stigma** around asking for help, **it would make a huge difference**.
開誠布公地談論這件事確實會對情況有所幫助。讓情況變好的其中一個方法是讓（心理諮商）治療變得更便宜。另外，如果我們能打破對於因為身心狀況而需要求助的恥辱感，那將帶來巨大的改變。

> **can take years** 可能需要數（十）年時間
> ❻ **It takes time** 這是需要時間的
> **It's a long process/journey** 會是漫長的過程

Healing from deep emotional wounds **takes time**—it's not something that **happens overnight**. Learning to let go **is a long journey**. You don't just wake up one day and feel completely fine.
從深層的情感傷痛中癒合需要時間，這不是一夕之間就能完成的事。學會放下是一段漫長的旅程，你不會某天醒來就突然感到完全沒事了。

> **put pressure on** 給……帶來壓力
> ❼ **carry a burden** 承受某種困難、壓力或負擔
> **make it harder for people to** 讓人們更難……

Everyone is **carrying a burden** we know nothing about.
每個人都背負著外人不了解的重擔。

House prices keep going up, and **it's putting a lot of pressure on young people**. **It makes it harder for them** to save enough for a down payment.
房價一直在漲,這讓年輕人壓力超大,也讓他們更難存到頭期款。

> **People already live in crisis** 人們早已生活在危機中
> ⑧ **live paycheck to paycheck** 月光族、手頭很緊
> **be caught up in** 被困住

People are caught up in financial struggles, barely making ends meet.
人們深陷財務困境,只能勉強維持最基本生活開銷。

With rising living costs, **more families are living paycheck to paycheck**.
隨著生活成本上漲,越來越多家庭只能勉強過日子。

> **That could soon affect us all** 可能很快就會影響到所有人
> ⑨ **sooner or later, this will hit us too** 遲早會對我們有影響
> **it's coming for all of us** 誰都逃不掉

We might think we're fine now, **but sooner or later, this will hit us too**.
我們現在可能覺得沒事,但遲早會影響到我們。

Death, **it's coming for all of us**.
死亡,誰都躲不過。

Notes

TOPIC 3

China's Dust Storm Crisis
沙塵暴挑戰

沙漠化　　　沙塵暴。

經濟成長

　　　　各種環境問題

嚴重到不僅影響中國
也波及到數千公里以外的國家

Reading

MP3 09

閱讀以下文章，粗體字部分是本文的關鍵短語，先想想它們的意思及用法，再跟著引導進行更多字彙擴充練習！

As China's remarkable economic growth continues, the country faces all kinds of environmental problems. One of the biggest is the yearly dust storms which blow across the country. **They pose a health risk**, cost businesses billions of dollars, and leave parts of the country coated in yellow dust. The problem is so severe that it's affecting China's neighbors as well as countries thousands of kilometers away.

The dust storm season lasts from March to May. Strong winds pick up dirt from the vast deserts and plains of northern and northwestern China and Mongolia. The dirt is then carried eastward across China. **Along the way**, **it mixes with** air pollution from factories. The toxic mix is then dumped on cities like Beijing and Tianjin. The storms then continue on, often dropping dust on Korea, Japan, and Taiwan. In fact, some storms move all the way across the Pacific Ocean, affecting the USA and Canada. The storms result in a number of problems. Cities are covered in layers of dust, so buildings, streets, and homes must be frequently cleaned. During serious storms, children, elderly people, and those with respiratory problems are advised to stay indoors. Schools and airports are sometimes closed, and poor visibility makes driving dangerous. Furthermore, when the storms cause factories to shut down, financial losses can be huge.

Although dust storms are **nothing new** in China, they have become more frequent and serious in recent years. A key reason is the overuse of land. Farmers work the land too intensively, weakening the soil. And China's massive livestock population – more than six billion animals – strips grasslands of their protective covering. In its weakened state, the soil is easily lifted by strong winds. Also, the lack of tree and grass cover makes it easier for deserts to spread. As a result, **the cycle of** dust storms grows even worse. China is taking steps to tackle this crisis. The top priority is to stop desertification by improving the strength of the soil. Under a government program which started in 2000, vast areas are being converted to grassland and woodland. The goal is to restore 205,000 square kilometers of land.

There is a pressing need to solve the problem soon. Millions of people have already been forced from their homes due to the spread of deserts. Many others, from China to Japan and beyond, are suffering from the yearly storms. Meeting the problem is a key test of China's ability to balance economic growth and environmental protection.

翻譯

隨著中國驚人的經濟成長持續發展，該國面臨著各種環境問題。其中一個最嚴重的問題是每年吹過全國的沙塵暴。這些沙塵暴不僅對健康構成威脅，讓企業損失數十億美元，並且使該國部分地區被黃色的塵土所覆蓋。這個問題嚴重到不僅影響中國，也波及到中國的鄰國及數千公里以外的國家。

沙塵暴季節從三月到五月。強風從中國北部、西北部和蒙古廣闊沙漠及平原捲起塵土，然後將塵土吹向中國東部。途中，這些塵土與來自工廠的空氣污染混合，形成有毒的混合物，最後飄到北京、天津等城市。沙塵暴接著繼續向東傳播，經常將塵土帶到韓國、日本和台灣。事實上，有些沙塵暴甚至會穿越整個太平洋，影響到美國和加拿大。這些沙塵暴造成了很多問題。城市被厚厚的灰塵覆蓋，建築物、街道和住宅需要經常清潔。當沙塵暴非常嚴重時，建議兒童、老年人和有呼吸道問題的人盡量待在室內。學校和機場有時會關閉，能見度差也讓開車變得危險。此外，當沙塵暴造成工廠停工時，財務損失也會非常巨大。

雖然沙塵暴在中國並不是什麼新鮮事，但近年來它們變得更加頻繁和嚴重。主要原因之一是土地過度使用。農民過度耕作土地，導致土壤日益貧瘠。而中國龐大的牲畜數量（超過六十億）也使草原失去保護層。土壤處於這種脆弱狀態時，很容易被強風捲起。此外，缺乏樹木和草地的覆蓋使得沙漠更容易擴展。因此，沙塵暴的循環變得更加惡化。中國正在採取措施應對這場危機。當前首要任務是透過強化土壤來遏制沙漠化。根據政府於 2000 年開始實行的計畫，大面積的土地被轉變為草原和森林。目標是要恢復 205,000 平方公里的土地。

這個問題越來越嚴重，亟需應對處理，目前已經有數百萬人因為沙漠化而被迫離開家園。從中國到日本甚至更遠的地方，許多人每年都深受沙塵暴之苦。如何解決這個問題，將會是中國在經濟成長與環境保護之間尋求平衡的一大挑戰。

Dust Storm Crisis

練習 A：用英文表達 Phrase in Action

用以下關鍵短語作為句子重點提示，試著用英文表達每一句話。不一定只有一種說法！

1 pose a health risk
空氣污染對所有年齡層的人都構成健康風險，尤其是對兒童影響更大。

2 There is a pressing need
為了在 2050 年達成淨零目標，迫切需要更嚴格的二氧化碳排放標準。

> 📎 1～2 這兩個短語用來描述某種問題的影響，其中 There is a pressing need 強調某事的緊迫性，常見於討論解決方案或政策時。

3 along the way
在這個過程中，工廠排放的污染物與車輛廢氣混合，形成濃霧，造成能見度降低。

4 it mixes with
當像是氮氧化物和二氧化硫這類污染物與空氣中的水和氧氣結合時，就會形成酸雨。

5 nothing new
霧霾在中國不是什麼新鮮事，但隨著煤炭產業和工業活動的成長，情況變得更糟。

> 📎 3～6 這些短語與某件事或某種現象的發展過程、狀態相關。

6 the cycle of
水的循環包括蒸發、凝結與降水。

Dust Storm Crisis

MP3 10

練習 B：記憶挑戰 *Phrase Recall!*

以下是練習 A 各句子的參考英文說法，但關鍵短語不見了！你還記得它的中文怎麼說嗎？

Reference Only – Not the Only Way!

1 (　　　　　　　)
Air pollution poses a health risk to people of all ages, but children are the most vulnerable.

2 (　　　　　　　　　)
To reach net zero by 2050, there is a pressing need for stricter CO_2 emission standards.

3 (　　　　　　　)
Along the way, pollutants from factories mix with vehicle emissions, creating a thick smog that reduces visibility.

4 (　　　　　　)
When pollutants like nitrogen oxide and sulfur dioxide mix with water and oxygen in the air, they form acid rain.

5 (　　　　　　)
Being blanketed with dense smog is nothing new in China, but it has worsened after a surge in coal burning and industrial activity.

6 (　　　　　　)
The cycle of water involves evaporation, condensation, and precipitation.

Let's Chat!

練習 C：靈活應用 Phrase Remix!
同樣的短語，放進生活其他情境中應用看看！
你也可以試著造自己的句子！

1 pose a health risk
舊建築中常見的材料，像是隔熱材料中的石棉、或是油漆當中的鉛，都對健康有危害。

2 There is a pressing need
在地震過後，迫切需要食物和水。

3 along the way
我們在自駕旅遊的一路上，遇到了很多善良的陌生人。

4 it mixes with
雨水積聚在街道上，與泥土和垃圾混合在一起，形成骯髒的水窪。

5 nothing new
這個社區每年雨季都會停電，這已經不是什麼新鮮事了。

6 the cycle of
死亡不是我們的敵人，它只是生命歷程的一部分。

Let's Chat!

MP3 11

練習 D：記憶挑戰 Phrase Recall!

以下是練習C各句子的參考英文說法，但關鍵短語不見了，而且還變長了！試著用你的話來描述這些被標示的語言段！

Reference Only – Not the Only Way!

1 (　　　　　　　　　　　　　)
Common materials found in old buildings, such as asbestos in insulation and lead in paint, can pose health risks.

2 (　　　　　　　　　　　　　)
After the earthquake, there is a pressing need for food and water.

3 (　　　　　　　　　　　　　)
We met many kind strangers along the way during our road trip.

4 (　　　　　　　　　　　　　)
When rainwater collects on the street, it mixes with mud and litter, creating dirty puddles.

5 (　　　　　　　　　　　　　)
The power outages in the neighborhood happen every year during the rainy season. It's nothing new.

6 (　　　　　　　　　　　　　)
Death isn't our enemy; it's just part of the cycle of life.

TOPIC ❸ 沙塵暴挑戰   43

Expand!（關鍵短語 1 + 1 > 2 !!）　　MP3 12

看看本單元學過的關鍵短語，還可以延伸出哪些相關說法呢？繼續擴充你的口說及寫作素材吧！

①
pose a health risk 有危害健康的風險
could lead to health problems 可能引發健康問題
put someone's life in danger 使某人的生命處於危險之中
put... at risk 讓……處於危險中

A: I've been working late this month. Gotta hustle to survive, right?
B: I get that. But don't overdo it. **That could lead to health problems**.
A：這個月我都在熬夜加班，真的是得拼命才活得下去，對吧？
B：我懂，不過別太過勉強自己，不然最後健康會出問題的。

A: I just don't get it! Why do people text while driving? Don't they know that it **puts other people's lives in danger**?
B: They either don't care or are just too careless to realize the risks.
A：我真不明白！為什麼有人會在開車時發簡訊？難道他們不知道這會把別人的生命置於危險中嗎？
B：他們要麼根本不在乎，要麼就是神經太大條，沒意識到這樣做很危險。

A: Last night, Jason gave me a ride home and he didn't have his seatbelt on.
B: Did you say something?
A: Of course, I told him "you're **putting your life and others at risk**", but he just laughed, saying I'm making a big deal out of it.
B: I didn't think he was that kind of person.
A：昨晚，Jason 載我回家，他竟然沒有繫安全帶。
B：你有說什麼嗎？
A：當然，我告訴他「你把自己的生命和別人的生命都置於危險中」，但他只是笑笑說我在小題大做。
B：我沒想到他會是這樣的人。

2
There is a pressing need 現在急需……
The situation calls for urgent action 情況迫切需要立刻有所行動
The clock is ticking 時間所剩無幾
We're at a crossroads 我們正面臨關鍵時刻

A: The hospital is running out of resources, and the emergency room is overcrowded.
B: **This situation calls for urgent action**; we need more doctors, healthcare staff, and supplies right away.
A：醫院資源快要耗盡，急診室也人滿為患。
B：我們應當立刻有所作為，首先需要增加醫護人員以及提供充足的醫療物資。

A: The deadline for the project is next week, and we still have so much to do.
B: Yeah, **the clock is ticking**, we need to speed up to finish everything on time.
A：專案的截止日期是下週，但我們還有好多事情沒做。
B：是啊，時間緊迫，我們得加快腳步才能按時完成。

A: We've been facing a tough time in sales.
B: I think **we're at a crossroads**. We need to decide whether to change our strategy or invest more in marketing..
A：我們最近業績非常不理想。
B：我認為我們現在正處於關鍵時刻，必須決定是要調整策略還是增加行銷預算。

TOPIC ❸ 沙塵暴挑戰

3
along the way 在過程中、一路上
on the way 在途中、在路上
as things unfold 隨著事情的發展、隨著情況的發展
to risk 冒險、置……於危險中

A: I stopped at a few places **along the way** to pick up some famous local snacks.
B: Oh, that sounds like a nice little detour!
A：我<u>在沿途幾個地方停下來</u>，買了一些當地有名的小吃特產。
B：哇，聽起來像是不錯的小插曲！

A: I'm not sure how the meeting will go, **but we'll see as things unfold**.
B: Yeah, we'll figure it out as we go along.
A：我不確定會議會怎麼進行，<u>但就看事態如何發展，我們再應變</u>。
B：對啊，我們就邊看之後情況如何，邊想辦法解決。

A: I'm thinking of skipping the safety precautions to finish the job faster.
B: If you do that, **you're not just risking your career** but everyone's safety too.
A：我在考慮要跳過安全措施，這樣可以更快完成工作。
B：如果這樣做，<u>你不只是拿你的職業生涯在賭</u>，你還拿大家的命在賭。

4
it mixes with 它與……混合
it blends with 它與……融合

A: When different paint colors **mix together**, you can get some really unexpected shades.
B: I know, I once tried to make purple and ended up with a weird brown.
A：當不同的顏料<u>混合在一起</u>時，可能會出現一些意想不到的色調。
B：真的，我有一次想說調調看紫色，結果卻變成了奇怪的咖啡色。

A: The new furniture **blends with** the style of the room perfectly.
B: Yeah, it looks like it belongs here.
A：新家具完美融入房間的設計。
B：沒錯，感覺就像本來就屬於這裡一樣。

> **5**
> **nothing new** 沒什麼新鮮的
> **just another day** 又是平凡的一天
> **business as usual** 一切照常
> **same old, same old** 老樣子

A: I heard that you're falling behind schedule again.
B: Oh, **nothing new**, that always happens.
A：我聽說你們又趕不上進度了。
B：喔，這不是新鮮事啊，一天到晚總是這樣的。

A: How was work today?
B: Just **another day at the office**, lots of meetings and emails.
A：今天工作怎麼樣？
B：又是平凡無奇的一天啊，開了很多會，回了很多信。

A: The factory was affected by the storm, but they're already back to work.
B: I guess **it's business as usual for them**.
A：工廠受到了暴風雨的影響，不過他們都已經回到崗位上工作了。
B：看來對他們來說，（儘管情況困難）一切照常運作。

A: How's everything going?
B: **Same old, same old**.
A：一切都還好嗎？
B：老樣子啊，沒什麼特別變化。

> **the cycle of** 循環
> ❻ **behavior pattern** 行為模式
> **get stuck in a loop** 陷入無限迴圈的困境

A: **The cycle of** seasons brings changes to the city's scenery every year.
B: Yeah, it's amazing to see how the city changes with each season.
A：每年季節的變換都帶來城市景色的變化。
B：是啊，隨著不同季節城市景色也不同，真的很棒。

A: Every time I try to do something for myself, my friend always guilt-trips me into changing my plans.
B: **That's her pattern of behavior! (That's typical of her.)** She always makes you feel bad for prioritizing yourself.
A：每次我自己有想做什麼事情，我的朋友總是用內疚感讓我改變計畫。
B：這就是她的一貫作風！她總是讓你因為優先考慮自己而感到愧疚。

A: You have to find a way out. **Or, you'll just get stuck in a stress loop.**
B: I know, but it's harder than I ever imagined.
A：你得找到方法改變這個情況，不然你就會一直困在壓力的惡性循環裡面。
B：我知道，但這比我想像的還要難。

TOPIC 4

Carbon Emissions
碳排放

碳補償　　　碳足跡。

低碳生活

全球挑戰

綠色能源
永續發展

森林保護計畫

碳中和

節能家電
油電混合車

碳排放標準

Reading

MP3 13

閱讀以下文章，粗體字部分是本文的關鍵短語，先想想它們的意思及用法，再跟著引導進行更多字彙擴充練習！

The threat caused by climate change is familiar to us all. Every day, we burn fossil fuels like coal and oil for energy. That releases tons of CO_2 into the air, leading to global warming, rising sea levels, and other serious problems. One way people, corporations, and governments are meeting the threat is by going carbon neutral. The idea is to release a net balance of zero CO_2. If enough people get involved, it could have a real impact in the fight to protect our planet.

Many of our daily activities produce CO_2. Driving, flying, using computers, and heating our homes **all add to the problem**. "Carbon calculators" can show you **how much CO_2 you are responsible for**. For example, flying from San Francisco to Tokyo releases almost one ton of CO_2 per person. Driving 20 kilometers to work produces around two tons per year. **Once you know** how much CO_2 you produce, **you can** start lowering your "carbon footprint." **That can be done by** buying energy-efficient light bulbs and home appliances like refrigerators and stoves. **By installing** solar panels, we can make our homes and businesses greener. Also, walking or riding a bicycle to work and driving hybrid cars all reduce CO_2 levels.

Even after **taking steps to** save energy, we still create some pollution. So the next step in going carbon neutral is to "offset" that amount. Offsetting means supporting energy-saving projects that balance out the CO_2 that you produce. Some examples are tree planting groups, solar energy efforts, and wind farms. **Let's say** your lifestyle produces 30 tons of CO_2. You could offset that total by giving money to a wind farm that produces the equivalent of 30 tons of clean energy. The net balance is zero.

Efforts to go carbon neutral are showing up everywhere. For example, the Olympics are now carbon neutral. So are some schools, like the College of the Atlantic. In the music industry, bands like the Rolling Stones are offsetting new CDs. Some people are even offsetting their weddings! Climate change is a matter of urgency. Many scientists say we need to lower CO_2 levels by 60% over the next 40 years. If we don't, there could be terrible consequences, both for the environment and the world economy. Though governments are talking about ways to lower pollution levels, these steps may not be enough. By going carbon neutral, individuals and businesses can do something meaningful to meet this global challenge.

翻譯

氣候變遷帶來的威脅我們都不陌生。每天，我們燃燒煤炭、石油等石化燃料來獲取能源，釋放出大量的二氧化碳進入大氣層，導致全球暖化、海平面上升，以及其他嚴重的環境問題。面對這樣的威脅，人們、企業與政府正努力朝向「碳中和」邁進。這個概念的核心是讓二氧化碳的淨排放量維持在零。如果有足夠多的人參與，將能為保護地球帶來實質影響。

我們的日常生活其實都在產生二氧化碳——開車、搭飛機、使用電腦，甚至是家中的暖氣設備都會增加碳排放量。「碳盤查計算器」可以幫助我們了解自己排放了多少二氧化碳。例如，從舊金山飛往東京，每人會產生將近一公噸的二氧化碳；每天開車通勤 20 公里，一年下來大約會排放兩公噸。當我們了解自己的碳排放量後，就可以開始減少「碳足跡」。例如，選擇購買省電燈泡與節能家電（如冰箱、爐具），或是透過安裝太陽能板，都可以使我們的家園和企業更加環保。此外，改用步行或騎腳踏車通勤，或是選擇油電混合車，這些也都能降低二氧化碳排放量。

然而，即使採取了節能措施，我們仍然會產生一些污染。因此，邁向碳中和的下一步，就是「碳補償」。所謂碳補償，就是透過支持節能或減碳計畫，來平衡自己所產生的碳排放量。例如，植樹計畫、太陽能發電專案，以及風力發電場等，都是常見方式。舉例來說，假設你的生活方式每年產生 30 公噸的二氧化碳，你可以捐款給風力發電場，讓它產生相當於 30 公噸的潔淨能源，這樣一來，你的碳排放「淨值」就會降為零。

如今，「碳中和」的概念已經在世界各地受到重視。例如，奧運會已經達成碳中和，部分學校（如大西洋學院）也是碳中和機構。在音樂產業中，像滾石樂隊這樣的知名樂團，他們的新專輯製作也加入了碳補償的機制。甚至有些人連婚禮都選擇能夠做到碳中和的方式來舉辦！氣候變遷已經是刻不容緩的問題。許多科學家警告，未來 40 年內，我們必須將二氧化碳排放量降低 60%，否則地球環境與全球經濟都必須面對嚴峻的後果。儘管各國政府正在討論如何減少污染，這些措施可能仍然不夠。因此，透過實踐碳中和，個人和企業可以為這場全球挑戰做出實質貢獻。

Carbon Emissions

練習 A：用英文表達 *Phrase in Acti*

用以下關鍵短語作為句子重點提示，試著用英文表達每一句話。不一定只有一種說法！

1 all add to the problem
訂外送、整天開著冷氣、還有一直買新衣服——這些看似平常的行為其實都會加劇碳排放的問題。

2 Once you know… you can…
一旦你知道自己的日常生活習慣會產生碳排放，你就可以開始做出一些小改變，例如減少開車次數，或多選擇本地食材。

3 how much CO_2 you are responsible for
你有沒有試著算一下自己每年會產生多少二氧化碳？「碳足跡計算器」可以給你一個數字，而結果可能會讓你大吃一驚！

4 let's say
假設你每天都買一杯外帶咖啡，那一年就會用掉 365 個一次性杯子。換成可重複使用的杯子可以減少許多垃圾量！

> 1～4 的短語用來描述問題的形成，舉實例解釋看似微不足道的行為如何會有好與壞的影響。

> 5～7 的短語用來描述具體行動與解決方案。

5 by doing something
改為使用節能燈泡，你可以省下電費，還能省錢。

6 that can be done by
減少免洗塑膠用品的垃圾其實很簡單，你可以隨身攜帶環保杯、購物袋和餐具。

7 taking steps to
越來越多人開始採取行動來減少碳足跡，比如少搭飛機、盡量搭乘大眾運輸，或是支持環保品牌。

Carbon Emissions

MP3 14

練習 B：記憶挑戰 Phrase Recall!

以下是練習 A 各句子的參考英文說法，但關鍵短語不見了！你還記得它的中文怎麼說嗎？

*Reference Only – Not the Only Way!

1（讓……問題更加嚴重）
Ordering delivery, keeping the AC on all day, and constantly buying new clothes all add to the problem of increasing carbon emissions.

2（　　　　　　　）
Once you know how your daily habits contribute to carbon emissions, you can start making small changes, like driving less or choosing local food.

3（　　　　　　　　　　　　　　）
Have you ever checked how much CO_2 you are responsible for each year? A carbon footprint calculator can give you a number, and the result might surprise you!!

4（　　　　　　　）
Let's say you grab a takeaway coffee every day, which adds up to 365 disposable cups a year. Switching to a reusable cup could reduce a lot of waste!

5（　　　　　　　　　　　）
By switching to energy-efficient light bulbs, you can save both electricity and money.

6（　　　　　　　）
Reducing your single-use plastic waste is easy. That can be done by carrying a reusable cup, shopping bags, and utensils whenever you go out.

7（　　　　　　　　　）
More people are taking steps to reduce their carbon footprint, like flying less, switching to public transport, and choosing sustainable brands.

TOPIC 4 碳排放

Let's Chat!

練習 C：靈活應用 **Phrase Remix!**
同樣的短語，放進生活其他情境中應用看看！
你也可以試著造自己的句子！

1 all add to the problem
A：我覺得大家工作上的壓力越來越大。
B：是啊，長時間工作、緊迫的截止日、缺乏支持——這些都讓過勞的問題更加嚴重。

2 Once you know... you can...
A：我一直說我要學做菜結果都沒學，可是現在我真的想試試看了。
B：這很棒啊！一開始會有點緊張是正常的，別擔心！只要掌握基本技巧後，你就可以隨心所欲做自己想吃的菜！

3 how much... you are responsible for
A：這週的待辦工作實在太多，讓我有點不知所措。
B：我通常會這麼做：先釐清狀況。等你看清楚每個環節，就會知道哪些是你該負責的，那就是你的優先順序。

4 Let's say
A：教授您好，感謝您今天的分享，不知道您能不能用簡單的例子來說明呢？
B：當然！假設你正在存旅遊基金。與其等到最後一刻才存錢，不如每週固定存 1000 元。你看，這就是設定小型短期目標的概念，當你堅持執行，這些小目標就會累積成大成果。

5 by doing...
A：最近我覺得工作壓力有點大。
B：你可以試著在休息時做一些簡單的放鬆運動，可能會感覺好一點。

6 that can be done by
A：我正在努力提高我的工作效率。
B：你可以每天早上列出待辦清單，這樣應該可以幫助你做事情更有條理。

7 taking steps to
A：Jeffery 最近怎麼樣？
B：很好啊，要謝謝你之前跟他聊過。他開始用「分段讀書」的方式在準備期末考，讓自己更專心。

Let's Chat!

MP3 15

練習 D：記憶挑戰 Phrase Recall!

以下是練習 C 各句子的參考英文說法，但關鍵短語不見了，而且還變長了！試著用你的話來描述這些被標示的語言段！

*Reference Only – Not the Only Way!

1 (　加劇……的問題　)
A: I think everyone's stress at work just keeps getting worse.
B: Yeah, long hours, tight deadlines, and high expectations all add to the problem of burnout.

2 (　　　　　　　　　　　　　　　)
A: I've been putting off learning how to cook, but I want to try it now.
B: Good for you! It's normal to feel a bit nervous at first, but don't worry! Once you know the basics, you can cook anything in your own way.

3 (　　　　　　　　　　　　　　　　　　　　　)
A: I'm feeling a bit overwhelmed with all the things I have to do this week.
B: Here's what I always do: take a closer look. Once you break it down, you'll see how much you're responsible for. That is your priority.

4 (　　　　　　　　　　　　　　　)
A: Thank you for sharing with us, Professor. I would like to ask if you could give us a simple example to make it easier to understand.
B: Sure! Let's say you're trying to save money for a trip. Instead of waiting until the last minute, you decide to set aside $1000 every week. See, it's about setting small, short-term goals, and when you stick to them, they can add up to something much bigger.

5 (　　　　　　　　　　　　　　　　　　　　　)
A: I've been feeling overwhelmed at work lately.
B: You might feel better by doing simple relaxation exercises during your breaks.

6 (　　　　　　　　　　)
A: I'm trying to be more productive at work.
B: That can be done by making a to-do list every morning.

7 (　　　　　　　　　　　　　)
A: How's Jeffery doing?
B: He's great. Thanks for talking to him. He is taking steps to prepare for his final exams by studying in shorter, focused sessions.

TOPIC 4 碳排放

Expand! (關鍵短語 1 + 1 > 2 !!)   MP3 16

看看本單元學過的關鍵短語，還可以延伸出哪些相關說法呢？繼續擴充你的口說及寫作素材吧！

> **1**
> **all add to the problem** 讓問題更嚴重
> **make things worse** 讓事情變得更糟
> **escalate** 讓情況或局勢惡化

The lack of communication, tight deadlines, and cross-cultural barriers **all add to the problem**. **To make things worse**, this year's bonus has been canceled. The stress within the team **has definitely escalated**.
缺乏溝通、緊迫的時間表和跨文化障礙，這些問題都讓情況變得更加嚴重，更糟的是，今年的獎金又被取消，整個團隊的壓力明顯加劇了。

> **2**
> **What you feel responsible for** 你覺得自己應該要承擔的
> **have something on your plate** 你手上的工作量
> **how much burden you're carrying** 你的負擔有多重

No one is a superhero. It's important to tell the difference between **what you feel responsible for** and what you can actually handle.
沒有人是超級英雄。分清楚你覺得你應該要承擔，和你實際上能負荷的差別，這很重要。

She's got a lot on her plate, with taking care of a newborn and three new projects.
她現在事情很多忙得不可開交，除了要照顧剛出生的寶寶，還有三個新項目在進行。

Sometimes it's hard to see **how much burden you're carrying** until you take a step back.
有時候你很難察覺自己承擔的負擔有多重，除非你退一步看看全局。

3
> **Once you know... you can...** 只要你知道……你就可以……
> **As soon as you figure out... you can...** 只要你弄清楚……你就可以……
> **Once you have a clear idea of... you'll be able to...**
> 只要你有更清楚的想法……你就能夠……

Once you know where to find the best deals, **you can** start saving a lot of money on your groceries.
只要你知道哪裡買東西最優惠，你就可以開始在買生活用品上省下很多錢。

As soon as you figure out how the new system works, **you can** complete the project much faster.
只要你弄清楚新系統怎麼運作，你就可以更快完成專案。

Once you have a clear idea of what you want, **you'll be able to** make better decisions.
只要你很清楚的知道自己想要什麼，你就能做出更好的決定。

4
> **Let's say** 假設……
> **what if** 如果……會怎麼樣……
> **imagine** 想像一下……

Let's say you've been thinking about changing careers, but you're not sure what's right. The first step is to get specific about what's not working.
假設你一直在考慮換工作領域，但不確定哪個選擇是對的。第一步是要清楚到底自己目前不滿意的地方在哪裡。

What if you could work remotely from anywhere in the world? **Imagine** being able to travel and explore new places while still being productive and earning a living.
要是你能在世界各地遠距工作會怎麼樣？想像一下這樣的生活，你可以在旅遊的同時，還能一邊工作賺錢。

⑤ That can be done by 這可以透過……來達成
You can make it happen 你可以做到這件事情

Wondering how to make your mornings less stressful? **That can be done by** preparing everything the night before.
早上忙不過來嗎？前一晚先準備好，一早起床就不會慌張了。

Want to get a good night's sleep? **You can make that happen** with our new memory foam pillow.
想要一夜好眠？有我們的新型記憶枕就能實現。

⑥ by doing something... 藉由做某件事情……
through doing something... 透過做某件事情……

You can put away clothes in minutes **by folding them right** after the dryer.
從烘乾機拿出來就馬上摺衣服，這樣幾分鐘內就能收好。

You can learn a lot **through interacting** with people from different cultures.
透過與來自不同文化的人互動，你可以學到很多東西。

⑦ taking steps to 採取措施來……
taking action to 採取行動來……

She is taking steps to improve her health by exercising regularly.
她正透過規律運動來改善健康。

They are taking action to address the environmental issues in their community.
他們正採取行動要設法解決社區中的環境問題。

Social Phenomena & Changes

社會現象與變遷

PART 2

TOPIC 5

Gossip Culture
八卦文化

點擊率
蹭。
帶風向
賺流量　瘋傳
釣魚式標題的誘惑

Reading

MP3 17

閱讀以下文章，粗體字部分是本文的關鍵短語，先想想它們的意思及用法，再跟著引導進行更多字彙擴充練習！

Are you curious about the private lives of actors and pop stars? If so, you're not alone. Every day, the world's newspapers, magazines, and websites deliver a constant stream of gossip about the rich and famous. Although it's sometimes called "junk food news," celebrity gossip is **more popular than ever**.

Movie stars, athletes, singers, and politicians are the favorite subjects of the **gossip media**. People feel very close to these superstars because they're always **in the public eye**. We want to know what they're doing, what clothes they're wearing, and who they're spending time with. In offices, chatrooms, and coffee shops, celebrity news is a common topic of conversation.

There's even a class of photographer, the "paparazzi," that follows celebrities around. Wherever stars eat, shop, or travel, the paparazzi are always there, cameras in hand. Some people see this as an **invasion of privacy**. But stars can benefit from the paparazzi, who sell their photos to news sources. This keeps stars in the public eye, which helps their careers.

Stories in the gossip media may be based on public facts, information from stars' friends, or secret "insider" sources. Regardless of how crazy the stories are, stars usually ignore them. Sometimes, however, they fight back. In Los Angeles and London, there are special lawyers who work for celebrities. They may sue a magazine for printing **a false story** or demand that photographs not be printed.

In today's world, the gossip media are everywhere. It's impossible for stars to hide from the press. Likewise, it's hard for the rest of us to avoid celebrity news. **At the end of the day**, we **have only ourselves**

to blame. As a famous magazine editor once said, celebrity gossip is everywhere because we **have such a huge appetite for it**.

翻譯

你對演員和流行歌手的私生活感到好奇嗎？如果是的話，你並不孤單。全球的報紙、雜誌和網站每天都持續不斷地傳遞有關富人和名人的八卦新聞。儘管這些有時被稱為「垃圾新聞」，但名人八卦如今比以往任何時候都更受歡迎。

電影明星、運動員、歌手和政治人物是八卦媒體最喜愛的話題。人們覺得與這些超級明星非常親近，因為他們總是出現在公眾的視線中。我們想知道他們在做什麼、穿什麼衣服以及和誰在一起。在辦公室、聊天室和咖啡店，名人新聞是常見的聊天話題。

甚至還有一類專門的攝影師──「狗仔隊」，專門跟拍名人。無論明星在哪裡吃飯、購物或旅行，狗仔隊總是手持相機出現在那裡。有些人認為這是對隱私的侵犯。但明星們也能從狗仔隊中受益，因為狗仔將他們的照片賣給新聞媒體，這讓明星留在公眾視線中，有助於他們的事業發展。

八卦媒體中的報導內容可能基於公開的事實、明星朋友的資訊，或者是祕密的「內部消息來源」。無論這些內容多麼荒誕，明星通常會選擇忽視它們。然而，有時他們會反擊。在洛杉磯和倫敦，有專門為名人工作的律師。他們可能會因為某雜誌刊登不實報導而提起訴訟，或者要求不要刊登某些照片。

在當今世界，八卦媒體無處不在。對於明星來說，想要躲避媒體幾乎是不可能的。同樣，我們一般人也很難避免接觸名人新聞。歸根究柢，我們只能怪自己。正如一位著名的雜誌編輯曾經說過，名人八卦無處不在，因為我們對它有著極大的渴望。

PLUS! 主題實用詞彙精選

- ☐ a stream of gossip 源源不絕的八卦
- ☐ celebrity gossip 名人八卦
- ☐ paparazzi culture 狗仔文化
- ☐ invasion of privacy 侵犯隱私
- ☐ insider sources 內部消息來源（知情人士透露）
- ☐ a huge appetite for 有對某事的食慾／渴望

Gossip Culture

練習 A：用英文表達 Phrase in Action

用以下關鍵短語作為句子重點提示，試著用英文表達每一句話。不一定只有一種說法！

1　more popular than ever
你有沒有注意到一件事，真人實境秀近來似乎比以往更受歡迎？

2　at the end of the day
到頭來，一切都跟錢有關。八卦是一門生意，而我們就是讓它活下去的那群人。

3　have only ourselves to blame
留言區充滿了負面情緒，我們卻還是忍不住點進去看。說到底也只能怪我們自己。

> 1～4 是強調結果的短語，適用於論述、解釋性文章或論證中，陳述某些現象或行為的結果或是影響。

4　have such a huge appetite for it
人們對八卦有著強烈的渴望，總是很難抵擋釣魚式標題的誘惑。

> 5～8 這些短語常用於談到媒體、隱私和公共生活有關的話題（例如侵犯隱私、八卦、假新聞等等）。

5　invasion of privacy
我也愛看明星八卦，但有些狗仔真的太誇張了，完全是侵犯隱私。

6　gossip media
八卦媒體最愛曲解你的話，編造故事來帶風向、賺流量、炒熱度。

7　in the public eye
處於公眾視野就像是生活在魚缸中一樣，這就是成名的代價。

8　a false story
造謠的內容幾分鐘就能被瘋傳，但是有誰真的在乎真相呢？

Gossip Culture

MP3 18

練習 B：記憶挑戰 **Phrase Recall!**

以下是練習A各句子的參考英文說法，但關鍵短語不見了！你還記得它的中文怎麼說嗎？
*Reference Only – Not the Only Way!

1 (比以往更受歡迎)
Have you ever noticed that reality shows seem to be more popular than ever?

2 ( )
At the end of the day, it all comes down to money. Gossip is a business, and we're the ones keeping it alive.

3 ( )
The comment sections are toxic, but we keep reading them. Honestly, we have only ourselves to blame.

4 ( )
People have such a huge appetite for gossip that they can't resist clickbait headlines.

5 ( )
I love celebrity gossip too, but some paparazzi go too far. It's a total invasion of privacy.

6 ( )
The gossip media often twist your words, make up stories, and stir the pot just to get more clicks.

7 ( )
Being in the public eye is like being a fish in a bowl. That's the unfortunate price of fame.

8 ( )
A false story can spread like wildfire online in no time, but who really cares about the truth?

TOPIC 5 八卦文化   65

Let's Chat!

練習 C：靈活應用 Phrase Remix!

同樣的短語，放進生活其他情境中應用看看！
你也可以試著造自己的句子！

1 more popular than ever
串流平台的受歡迎程度前所未有。
有線電視還有人在看嗎？

2 at the end of the day
說到底，人都希望能夠被看見、
被聽見、被理解。

3 have only ourselves to blame
當事情出了差錯，我們往往會怪罪他人或其他外在因素。但其實，
很多時候，問題就出在我們自己身上。

4 have a huge appetite for it
最近為什麼超級想吃垃圾食品？我猜可能是因為壓力太大。

5 invasion of privacy
沒經過同意就去看另一半的手機？
這是侵犯隱私啊！

6 gossip media
不管你喜不喜歡，八卦媒體都是個數十億美元的產業，
因為醜聞能賣錢，狗血劇情帶來流量。

7 in the public eye
一旦走紅，不管你願不願意，
你都會活在公眾視野裡。

8 a false story
假新聞和不實報導究竟能有多大的
殺傷力？等我們發現的時候，通常
已經為時已晚。

Let's Chat!

MP3 19

練習 D：記憶挑戰 *Phrase Recall!*

以下是練習 C 各句子的參考英文說法，但關鍵短語不見了，而且還變長了！試著用你的話來描述這些被標示的語言段！

*Reference Only – Not the Only Way!

1 (   )
Streaming services are more popular than ever. Is cable TV a thing of the past?

2 (   )
At the end of the day, we all just want to feel seen, heard, and understood.

3 (   )
When things fall apart, we tend to point the finger at someone or something. But often, we have only ourselves to blame.

4 (   )
Why do I have a huge appetite for junk food lately? I guess it's probably because of all the stress.

5 (   )
Going through your partner's phone without consent? That's an invasion of privacy!

6 (   )
Like it or not, the gossip media are a billion-dollar industry. Scandals sell, and drama drives clicks.

7 (   )
Once you go viral, you're in the public eye whether you like it or not.

8 (   )
How damaging can false stores and fake news really be? By the time we realize what's happening, it's often too late.

TOPIC ⑤ 八卦文化   67

Expand! （關鍵短語 1 + 1 > 2 !!）

MP3 20

看看本單元學過的關鍵短語，還可以延伸出哪些相關說法呢？繼續擴充你的口說及寫作素材吧！

> **1** **invasion of privacy** 侵犯隱私
> **cross the line** 行為／話語越過界限，沒禮貌、不恰當、不尊重
> **way over the line** 非常沒品、十分惡劣

Posting a tribute to a celebrity who passed away? That's just showing respect—it has nothing to do with **invasion of privacy**. Digging up dirt on them, or speculating about their cause of death for clicks? Now that's **crossing the line**.

發文悼念一位去世的名人？這只是對他的離世表達關注，與侵犯隱私無關。但是去爆人家黑料或是隨便臆測死因，只為了賺流量？這就太超過了。

Using their name as a hashtag to promote your merchandise? That's **way over the line**.

用他們的名字作為一個 # 話題標籤來推廣自己的商品？這太惡劣了。

> **2** **in the public eye** 公眾注目
> **in the spotlight** 鎂光燈下（備受關注）
> **under the spotlight** 被仔細檢視（通常有壓力）

Celebrities nowadays can be anyone—from a TikToker to a reality TV star. The moment they go viral, they **step into the spotlight**. Like it or not, living **in the public eye** is part of the deal. And if they mess up, they'll quickly find themselves **under the spotlight**, with the whole world digging into their past.

現在，任何人都有可能是名人，從 TikTok 網紅到真人實境秀明星，只要爆紅，就會備受關注。不管喜不喜歡，眾人的眼光就是會隨著名氣而來。而如果他們出了什麼差錯，很快就會被放大檢視，全世界都盯著他們，翻舊帳、挖黑歷史。

> **gossip media** 八卦媒體
> ❸ **tabloid journalism** 小報新聞
> **clickbait news** 釣魚式新聞標題

Tabloid journalism, **gossip media**, and **clickbait news** work together to spin stories, exaggerate facts, and keep people hooked.
小報新聞、八卦媒體和釣魚式新聞標題互相配合，編造故事、誇大事實，就是要讓你追不停。

> **have only ourselves to blame** 只能怪我們自己
> ❹ **It's on us** 這得由我們來承擔、這算在我們頭上
> **learn something the hard way** 吃了苦頭才學到教訓

We messed up, and we **have only ourselves to blame**. **It's on us**. But honestly, if we had just listened to him back then, things would have been so much easier. Guess we just had to **learn that the hard way**.
我們搞砸了，這只能怪自己，現在只能靠我們來收拾。但說真的，如果當初我們有聽他的勸告，事情就會簡單很多。看來我們非得吃點苦頭才學得會啊。

> **have a huge appetite for it** 對它有強烈的興趣／慾望
> ❺ **Can't get enough of** 超愛、怎麼都不會膩
> **endlessly scrolling through** 滑手機滑個不停

People are obsessed with mindless entertainment. They can't stop watching memes, reaction videos, and ASMR, **endlessly scrolling through** Reels, TikToks, and Shorts. Why? Short videos just draw you in before you even realize it.
人們對無腦娛樂著迷不已。他們無法停止觀看迷因、反應影片和 ASMR，無止境地滑動 Reels、TikTok 和 Shorts。為什麼？因為短影片總是能不知不覺地吸引你。

> **a false story** 假新聞、不實報導
> ❻ **misinformation** 錯誤資訊
> **media manipulation** 媒體操弄

A false story isn't just **misinformation**. The problem is that **media manipulation** can spread mistrust, distort facts, and shape opinions.
假新聞不僅僅是錯誤資訊而已。問題在於，媒體操弄能夠挑撥離間、扭曲事實，並影響公眾認知。

> **at the end of the day** 說到底
> ❼ **bottom line** 最重要的是、本質
> **what really matters** 真正重要的是

At the end of the day, the **bottom line** is being true to yourself. That's **what really matters**.
說到底，最重要的事情就是要坦承面對自己。

TOPIC 6

Culture Without Borders
世界地球村

地球村。

好萊塢

日本動漫

物流

Reading

MP3 21

閱讀以下文章，粗體字部分是本文的關鍵短語，先想想它們的意思及用法，再跟著引導進行更多字彙擴充練習！

With the growth of the Internet, tourism, and the global economy, **it feels like** the world is getting smaller. Ideas, products, and customs are flying from country to country **in the blink of an eye**. As these cultural exports grow, the world is slowly but surely becoming a global village.

Entertainment is one of the most popular cultural exports. Every year, movies from Hollywood are watched by billions of people worldwide. Likewise, **TV shows and music are making their way from America to Asia**. As people enjoy these entertainment products, they also learn about the ideas and values of other cultures.

Books can give an even deeper insight into a foreign country's history and beliefs. Novels from South America, Asia, and Africa have been translated into many languages. For younger readers, the *Harry Potter* novels from England **as well as** comics from Japan **are examples of** very successful exports.

Food is a tasty way for the world's cultures to meet up. For more than 100 years, Chinese immigrants have opened restaurants from London to Rio. Likewise, Indian and Arabic food can be found in most major cities. When we eat at these places, new words like "nan" and "falafel" enter our vocabulary. Then, of course, there's fast food. Though unhealthy, it certainly is popular.

Fashion is another big cultural export. In the past, it took months for trends to spread to other countries. Now, with the Internet, a new style from Paris can **become famous overnight**. Plus, today's super-fast shipping means that a shop in South Africa can receive European goods in no time.

Some people are unhappy about the rapid spread of foreign cultures. They worry it will harm their local identity. For sure, young people are often interested in new ideas and products from abroad. Yet **the more we learn about each other, the closer we become**. That helps export our most important cultural products: greater understanding and world peace.

翻譯

隨著網際網路、觀光旅遊和全球經濟的發展，世界似乎變得越來越小。各種想法、產品和風俗習慣能夠瞬間從一個國家傳播到另一個國家。隨著這些文化輸出的增長，世界正慢慢但確實地朝向「地球村」的方向發展。

娛樂是最受歡迎的文化輸出之一。每年，來自好萊塢的電影吸引全球數十億觀眾。同樣地，美國的電視節目和音樂也逐漸傳播到亞洲。當人們享受這些娛樂產品時，也同時在接觸與學習其他文化的思想與價值觀。

書籍能讓我們更深入了解異國的歷史與信仰。來自南美洲、亞洲和非洲的小說已被翻譯成多種語言。對於年輕讀者來說，來自英國的《哈利波特》系列以及來自日本的漫畫，都是非常成功的文化輸出例子。

美食則是一種讓世界文化相互交融的美味方式。百年來，來自中國的移民在全球各地從倫敦到里約熱內盧開設餐館。同樣，印度料理與阿拉伯料理如今在大多數主要城市都能找到。當我們在這些餐廳用餐時，像 nan「烤餅」和 falafel「鷹嘴豆丸子」等詞彙也悄悄融入我們日常語言之中。而談到全球飲食文化，當然少不了速食，雖然不太健康，但它確實在全球廣受歡迎。

時尚也是重要的文化影響力之一。在過去，新的潮流往往需要數個月才能傳播到其他國家。但如今，透過網際網路，來自巴黎的時尚風格可以在一夜之間風靡全球。此外，如今超快速的物流讓南非的商店能夠在短時間內就收到來自歐洲的商品，使時尚流動更加無國界。

然而，有些人對於外國文化的快速傳播感到不安，擔心這可能會對本土文化認同產生威脅。的確，年輕人往往對來自國外的新觀念和產品更感興趣。然而，彼此了解得越多，我們的距離就越近。而這也幫助我們出口最重要的文化產品：增進理解和世界和平。

Culture Without Borders

練習 A：用英文表達 Phrase in Action

用以下關鍵短語作為句子重點提示，試著用英文表達每一句話。不一定只有一種說法！

1 it feels like
如果你走在台北街頭，你會發現拉麵店、義式咖啡館和韓式燒烤都在同一條街上。這感覺就像是一次不需要護照的旅行。

> 📎 表達比較或關聯性：
> 1～4 這些短語用來比較、說明事物之間的關係，或提供例子來支持論點。

2 as well as
K-pop 現在已經是個幾十億美元的產業了。它融合了西洋流行、嘻哈，還有韓國自己的傳統音樂風格。

3 are examples of
手搖飲和拉麵店在全球各地興起，正是亞洲美食風靡全球的最佳例證。

4 the more…, the closer…
我們對不同文化了解得越多，就越能與世界各地的人拉近距離。

5 in the blink of an eye
在社群媒體的推波助瀾下，一個巴西小男孩的跳舞影片，可能一夜之間就變成文化潮流！全世界都知道了。

6 making their way from America to Asia
像漢堡店和咖啡店這類連鎖餐飲品牌紛紛從美國進軍亞洲，但它們也根據當地口味做了調整。

> 📎 表達時間或變化：
> 5～7 這些短語與時間的推移、變化的過程或某事迅速發生有關。

7 become famous overnight
某位不知名攝影師的推文被轉發了好幾十萬次，就這樣，他一夜成名。

Culture Without Borders

MP3 22

練習 B：記憶挑戰 Phrase Recall!

以下是練習 A 各句子的參考英文說法，但關鍵短語不見了！你還記得它的中文怎麼說嗎？

Reference Only – Not the Only Way!

1 (　感覺就好像是　)
If you walk around Taipei you'll see ramen shops, Italian cafés, and Korean barbecue all on the same street. It feels like a passport-free trip.

2 (　　　　　　)
K-pop has become a multi-billion-dollar industry. It blends influences from Western pop and hip-hop, as well as Korea's own traditional music.

3 (　　　　　　)
Bubble tea and ramen shops popping up worldwide are examples of how Asian cuisine has become a global phenomenon.

4 (　　　　　　)
The more we learn about different cultures, the closer we feel to people from around the world.

5 (　　　　　　　　　)
With the help of social media, a dance video from a child in Brazil could become a cultural trend in the blink of an eye. Suddenly, it's a global thing.

6 (　　　　　　　　　　)
Food chains like burger joints and coffee shops have made their way from America to Asia, but they've also adapted to local tastes.

7 (　　　　　　　　　　)
A tweet from an unknown photographer was retweeted hundreds of thousands of times, and just like that, he became famous overnight.

TOPIC 6 世界地球村

Let's Chat!

練習 C：靈活應用 Phrase Remix!

同樣的短語，放進生活其他情境中應用看看！
你也可以試著造自己的句子！

1 it feels like
自從有了外送平台，好像那些有名的餐廳都近在咫尺一樣。

2 as well as
她不僅是個超棒的廚師，也很會說故事，
所以去她家吃飯從來不只是為了食物。

3 are examples of
忘記別人的生日和不回訊息，都是可能傷害友誼的例子。

4 the more..., the...
你越是逃避問題，之後想要解決就會變得越困難。

5 in the blink of an eye
我想說我就只是滑一下 IG 限動，結果就才一眨眼的時間而已，
兩個小時就過去了。

6 making their way from... to...
珍珠奶茶最早來自台灣，但現在已經風靡全球，
從亞洲一路紅到美國，甚至到更遠的地方。

7 become famous overnight
他睡前發了一支搞笑影片，結果一覺醒來就破百萬觀看次數，
可謂一夜成名。

Let's Chat!

MP3 23

練習 D：記憶挑戰 Phrase Recall!

以下是練習C各句子的參考英文說法，但關鍵短語不見了，而且還變長了！試著用你的話來描述這些被標示的語言段！

Reference Only – Not the Only Way!

1 (　　　　　　)
Thanks to food delivery apps, it feels like all those popular restaurants are just a tap away.

2 (　　　　　　)
She's a great cook as well as an amazing storyteller, so dinner at her place is never just about food.

3 (　　　　　　)
Forgetting someone's birthday and not replying to messages are examples of things that can hurt a friendship.

4 (　　　　　　)
The more you try to avoid a problem, the harder it becomes to deal with later.

5 (　　　　　　)
I thought I was just scrolling through my friends' IG stories, and in the blink of an eye, two hours had passed.

6 (　　　　　　)
Bubble tea started in Taiwan, but now it's everywhere, making its way from Asia to America and beyond.

7 (　　　　　　)
He posted a funny video before going to bed, and when he woke up, he had a million views—he became famous overnight.

TOPIC 6 世界地球村　77

Expand! (關鍵短語 1 + 1 > 2 !!)

看看本單元學過的關鍵短語，還可以延伸出哪些相關說法呢？繼續擴充你的口說及寫作素材吧！

> **①**
> **it feels like** 感覺就像……
> **It gives me the feeling that...** 讓我覺得……
> **It reminds me of...** 讓我想到、想起……

It feels like I never left this place. The scent of wooden floors is exactly the same. **It's as if time stood still**. **It gives me the feeling that** I could turn a corner and see my younger self playing in the living room. **It reminds me of the days** when I would sit by the window, reading for hours, not a care in the world.

感覺自己從未離開過這裡，木地板的味道一樣沒變，時間彷彿在這裡靜止。走過轉角的瞬間，我幾乎以為，我會看到童年的自己在客廳裡玩耍。這讓我想起了那些日子，我常坐在窗邊，書一讀就是好幾個小時，什麼煩惱也沒有。

> **②**
> **in the blink of an eye** 轉眼間
> **almost without realizing it** 幾乎沒意識到
> **before you know it...** 一轉眼就、不知不覺中

In the blink of an eye, the kids who once played in the backyard are now packing their bags for college. **Before you know it**, they'll be building lives of their own, chasing dreams in cities far from home. And one day, **almost without realizing it**, you'll be the one waiting for their calls on Sunday nights.

一轉眼，曾經在後院玩耍的孩子，如今收拾行囊準備離家上大學。再一眨眼，他們已經遠離家鄉，有了自己的生活，追逐各自的夢想。而某一天，你才猛然發現，不知從何時開始，自己變成了那個在週日夜晚，默默等待手機鈴聲響起的人。

as well as 以及、僅⋯⋯還有⋯⋯
❸ **along with...** 加上、連同
together with... 與⋯⋯一起

The concert had a famous rock band, **as well as some rising indie artists**. **Along with an incredible light show and stage effects**, the event became a night to remember. **Together with thousands of passionate fans**, the energy in the arena was absolutely electric.
這場演唱會不僅有知名搖滾樂團演出，還邀請了幾位新崛起的獨立音樂人。搭配上震撼的燈光和舞台特效，整場演出精彩萬分，成為令人難忘的夜晚。現場數千名熱情的觀眾聚在一起，氣氛嗨到最高點，震撼無比。

❹ **are examples of** 就是⋯⋯的例子、是⋯⋯的典範
serve as a perfect example of... 作為⋯⋯的完美範例

Movies like *The Shawshank Redemption* and *Schindler's List* **are great examples of how films can** tell powerful stories and make people reflect on human nature. In particular, *Schindler's List* **serves as a perfect example of** how storytelling can bring history to life and leave a lasting impact.
像《刺激1995》和《辛德勒的名單》這樣的電影，正是展現電影如何震撼人心並讓人思考人性的絕佳範例。其中，《辛德勒的名單》是個很好的例子，讓我們看到故事如何讓歷史活過來，並對觀眾產生深遠的影響。

the more..., the closer... 越⋯⋯，⋯⋯就越靠近
❺ **the sooner..., the better...** 越快⋯⋯，⋯⋯就越好
the more..., the less... 越⋯⋯，反而越⋯⋯

The more time you spend with someone, **the closer** you become.
你花在一個人身上的時間越多，彼此的感情就會越深。

The sooner you talk about your issues, **the better** your relationship will be.
你越早敞開心扉，關係就會越融洽。

TOPIC ❻ 世界地球村

The more you try to please everyone, **the less happy** you'll be.
你越想討好所有人，反而會越不快樂。

> making their way from... to...　從……流行到、擴展到……
> **⑥ become a global phenomenon**　成為全球熱潮
> crossing cultural boundaries...　跨越文化界線、打破文化隔閡

K-pop was initially a music subculture in South Korea back in the 90s. Now it's pretty much everywhere. When BTS or BLACKPINK drop a new song, fans go straight to social media with edits, dance covers, and memes. People often talk about **how it has become a global phenomenon**. But honestly, it's more than that. **It crossed cultural boundaries** and brought people from different cultures together through music.

K-pop 一開始是 90 年代在韓國興起的一種小眾文化。而現在基本上已經紅遍全世界了。每當 BTS 或 BLACKPINK 一出新歌，粉絲們馬上衝上社群媒體發影片、翻唱翻跳和各種迷因。大家常在討論，K-pop 是如何成為全球風靡的熱潮的，但說實話，這不僅如此。它突破了文化界限，透過音樂將不同文化的人們聯繫在一起。

> **⑦ become famous overnight**　一夜成名
> **blow up overnight**　爆紅

He spent ten years doing stand-up at open mics with small audiences. Eventually, reality hit him hard, and he decided to quit. Right after he made that decision, he thought, "Why not post one last video on TikTok?" Who would've predicted it? That video went viral with millions of views, and his social media **blew up overnight** with likes, comments, and booking requests.

他花了十年時間四處表演脫口秀，每次面對的觀眾都不多。最終，夢想敵不過現實，他決定要放棄了。就在做出這個決定後，他想，「不如就在 TikTok 上發最後一支影片好了！」誰能想得到，那支影片竟然爆紅，獲得了數百萬次觀看，他的社群媒體一夜之間被數以萬計的按讚、留言和演出邀約淹沒。

TOPIC 7

Aging Society
高齡社會

老化。
沉重壓力

出生率下降

社會問題

壽命延長

Reading

MP3 25

閱讀以下文章，粗體字部分是本文的關鍵短語，先想想它們的意思及用法，再跟著引導進行更多字彙擴充練習！

Many countries **are going through** an important population shift. People are having fewer children, and lifespans are getting longer. The result is an average population age that keeps going up. The situation is creating serious problems.

Low fertility rates are the first key to the aging population issue. In most developed countries, the rate has fallen over the last 50 years. For example, in South Korea, it went from 6.16 in 1960 to 1.30 in 2012. Taiwan's rate fell from around 5.00 in 1960 to 1.27 in 2012. These numbers are above their **all-time** lows. However, a country needs a fertility rate of 2.10 to keep its population stable.

Longer lifespans are the second key. With better healthcare and nutrition, we're living **longer than ever**. For example, in 2012 the average lifespan in Brazil was 77 years for women and 70 for men. In Egypt, the average that same year was 73 for women and 69 for men. These numbers are climbing and could reach 100 **in the coming decades**.

Living longer is great, but it leads to some problems. After people retire, they collect pensions, and their healthcare costs go up. **Much of the burden** for paying these costs **falls on** the current workforce. Yet as the workforce gets smaller (due to lower fertility rates), less tax money is collected. The situation puts heavy pressure on companies and governments.

To make up for these losses, some governments are encouraging people to have more children. Also, robots are being built to work in offices and provide healthcare. Finally, through immigration, countries like England and the USA are adding to their workforce.

Some countries are **in a rush** to find answers. In Japan, about 25% of the population is 65 or older. That will likely climb to over 30% by 2030. Other countries, like Germany and Italy, are facing similar situations. **Time will tell** which methods can successfully deal with our aging populations.

翻譯

許多國家正面臨重大的人口變化──人們生育的孩子越來越少，壽命卻越來越長，導致人口平均年齡持續上升，這種情況正引發嚴重的問題。

低生育率是人口老化的首要因素。在大多數已開發國家，出生率在過去 50 年大幅下降。例如，韓國的出生率從 1960 年的 6.16 降至 2012 年的 1.30，台灣則從 5.00 降至 1.27。雖然這些數據略高於歷史最低點，但要維持人口穩定，生育率至少需要達到 2.10。

人均壽命延長也是關鍵因素之一。醫療與營養的進步讓人們活得更久，例如 2012 年巴西女性平均壽命達 77 歲，男性為 70 歲，而埃及則為女性 73 歲、男性 69 歲。這些數據仍在上升，在未來數十年內，甚至可能突破 100 歲。

儘管長壽是值得慶祝的好事，但它也帶來了一系列的挑戰。年長者在退休之後，需要領取養老金，而醫療支出也隨之增加，這些費用的重擔落在目前勞動人口身上，然而，隨著勞動人口因低生育率而縮減，稅收減少，政府和企業因此面臨更沉重的壓力。

為因應這些問題帶來的影響，各國開始採取不同的措施──鼓勵生育、發展機器人來協助辦公室工作並提供醫療照護，甚至透過移民來補足勞動市場的需求。英國與美國便透過移民政策來增加勞動力。

一些國家正迫切尋求解決方案。例如，在日本，65 歲以上的老年人口已佔總人口的 25%，預計到 2030 年，這個比例將會超過 30%。德國與義大利等國也面臨類似挑戰。未來，究竟哪種方法能真正有效因應人口老化問題，時間將會給出答案。

PLUS! 主題實用詞彙精選

- ☐ population shift 人口變化
- ☐ average lifespan 平均壽命
- ☐ fertility rate 生育率
- ☐ all-time low 歷史新低點
- ☐ keep something stable 保持穩定、不波動的狀態
- ☐ to make up for 彌補、補償

Aging Society

練習 A：用英文表達 Phrase in Acti

用以下關鍵短語作為句子重點提示，試著用英文表達每一句話。不一定只有一種說法！

1 be going through
許多國家正經歷重大的人口變遷，出生率下降，人均壽命延長。

2 in the coming decades
在未來幾十年內，許多國家 60 歲以上人口將超過勞動年齡人口。

3 time will tell
有些國家依靠移民，另一些則投入人工智慧來因應勞動力短缺的問題。唯有時間能證明哪種方式最有效。

> 📎 1～3 這些短語描述背景、推論未來，並在結尾時保持一個開放性的討論空間。

4 all-time
該國的出生率已降至歷史新低，使得維持穩定的勞動力變得困難。

> 📎 4～7 這些片語強調某種狀態或程度，如 "all-time" 用於表達最高或最低的紀錄，"in a rush" 描述匆忙的狀態，而 "than ever" 用於比較過去與現在的差異。

5 比較級 + than ever
隨著醫療技術的進步，人們的壽命比以往任何時候都更長，但這也加劇了人口老化的問題。

6 much of the burden falls on
支撐老齡人口的負擔，很大一部分落在年輕勞動者身上，他們需要繳納更高的稅金與提撥更多退休金。

7 in a rush
許多政府正急於尋找解決人口老化危機的方法，但這不是一朝一夕能解決的問題。

練習 B：記憶挑戰 Phrase Recall!

以下是練習A各句子的參考英文說法，但關鍵短語不見了！你還記得它的中文怎麼說嗎？

Reference Only – Not the Only Way!

1 (　　　　　　　)
Many countries are going through major demographic changes as birth rates drop and people live longer.

2 (　　　　　　　　　)
In the coming decades, the number of people aged 60 years and older will outnumber the working age population in many countries.

3 (　　　　　　　)
Some countries are relying on immigration, while others invest in AI to deal with labor shortages. Only time will tell which approach works best.

4 (　　　　　　　)
The country's birth rate has hit an all-time low, making it difficult to maintain a stable workforce.

5 (　　　　　　　)
With medical advancements, people are living longer than ever, but this also means a rapidly aging population.

6 (　　　　　　　　　　)
Much of the burden for supporting an aging population falls on younger workers through higher taxes and pension contributions.

7 (　　　　　　　)
Many governments are in a rush to find solutions for the aging crisis, but there's no quick fix.

Let's Chat!

練習 C：靈活應用 Phrase Remix!
同樣的短語，放進生活其他情境中應用看看！
你也可以試著造自己的句子！

1 be going through
你的好朋友看起來壓力很大，所以你問：
「嘿，你還好嗎？感覺你最近壓力很大，有很多事情。」

2 in the coming decades
在一部紀錄片中，科學家說：
「時間已經不多了，在未來幾十年內，氣候變遷將徹底改變我們的日常。」

3 time will tell
在新關稅實施後，記者寫道：
「很多人認為新的關稅會導致通膨上升，並對全球經濟造成傷害，到底結果如何，時間會證明一切。」

4 all-time
聽完這張專輯你就會懂，難怪它會成為史上最暢銷的專輯。

5 比較級 + than ever
談論人工智慧與科技時，有人說：
「科技發展的速度比以往任何時候都更快。十年前，我們根本無法想像今天的技術。」

6 much of the burden falls on
在團隊會議中，你的主管說：
「這個專案的重責大任落在行銷團隊身上，所以我們要確保他們得到足夠的支援。」

7 in a rush
你在課堂上，看到你的同學很疲憊，不斷打哈欠。
你問：「你還好嗎？」他回答：「早上趕得要命，我連咖啡都沒時間買。」

Let's Chat!

MP3 27

練習 D：記憶挑戰 Phrase Recall!

以下是練習C各句子的參考英文說法，但關鍵短語不見了，而且還變長了！試著用你的話來描述這些被標示的語言段！

Reference Only – Not the Only Way!

1 (　　　　　　　　　)
Your best friend looks stressed, so you ask:
"Hey, are you okay? You look like you're going through a lot right now."

2 (　　　　　　　　　)
A scientist in a documentary says:
"In the coming decades, climate change will drastically affect our daily lives. We're running out of time."

3 (　　　　　　　　　)
After the new tariffs are implemented, a journalist writes:
"A lot of people say the new tariffs will drive up inflation and hurt economies worldwide. Only time will tell."

4 (　　　　　　　　　)
Once you listen to the album, you can't help but think,
"No wonder it's an all-time bestseller."

5 (　　　　　　　　　)
Talking about AI and technology, someone says:
"Technology is advancing faster than ever. Ten years ago, we couldn't even imagine what we have today."

6 (　　　　　　　　　)
In the team meeting, your manager says:
"Much of the burden for this project falls on the marketing team, so let's make sure they get all the support they need."

7 (　　　　　　　　　)
You're in class with your classmate, and he looks tired, yawning repeatedly. You ask, "Are you alright?" He responds, "I didn't have time to grab a coffee. I was in a rush this morning."

TOPIC 7 高齡社會   87

Expand! （關鍵短語 1 + 1 > 2 !!）　　　MP3 28

看看本單元學過的關鍵短語，還可以延伸出哪些相關說法呢？繼續擴充你的口說及寫作素材吧！

❶　**be going through** 正在經歷 / 面對困難
　　be struggling with 正在掙扎於 / 面臨困難
　　be facing/experiencing 正面臨 / 正經歷著

She's going through a tough time after losing her job, but she's trying to stay positive.
她失業之後，正經歷一段低潮時期，但仍努力保持樂觀的心態。

He's struggling with math and might need a tutor.
他數學讀得很吃力，可能需要請家教幫忙。

The company is facing financial difficulties and may have to lay off employees.
這家公司正面臨財務困難，可能得裁員。

We are experiencing some delays due to technical issues, but we appreciate your patience.
由於技術問題，處理的進度會稍微延誤，感謝您的耐心等候。

❷　**stronger/faster/bigger than ever** 比以往更強 / 更快 / 更大
　　be better off（經濟狀況）比以前好

Now that we're both working, we're definitely **better off**.
現在我們是雙薪，經濟狀況當然比以前好很多。

This year's hurricane is **stronger than ever**, causing massive damage.
今年的颶風來勢洶洶，造成嚴重損害。

3 **in the coming decades** 在未來幾十年內
in the foreseeable future 在可預見的未來

In the foreseeable future, self-driving cars are expected to become a common sight.
在可預見的未來，無人駕駛汽車有望成為一件稀鬆平常的事情。

4 **time will tell** 時間會證明
we'll see in the future 未來我們就會知道結果
let's wait and see 拭目以待、靜觀其變
what happens next / how things unfold 接下來會發生什麼 / 事情如何發展

Only time will tell if their new business strategy will actually work.
只有時間能證明他們新的策略是否真的有效。

We'll see in the future whether AI can truly replace human creativity.
未來我們會知道人工智慧是否真的能取代人類的創造力。

They're facing some setbacks, **but let's wait and see how things unfold**.
他們遇到了一些挫折，不過我們就先靜觀其變吧。

The company is making big changes, and we're all curious about **what happens next**.
這家公司正在進行重大變革，我們都很好奇接下來會發生什麼事情。

5 **all-time** 歷來、史上
unprecedented 前所未有的
greatest of all time (GOAT) 史上最偉大的

This year's heatwave **has reached an all-time high**, breaking temperature records across the country.
今年的熱浪達到了歷史新高，打破了全國各地的氣溫紀錄。

The team's comeback in the final minutes was **unprecedented**; no one had ever seen anything like it.
球隊在最後幾分鐘的逆轉堪稱史無前例,沒有人見過這樣的比賽。

Many consider him **the greatest of all time** when it comes to basketball.
在籃球界,許多人認為他是史上最偉大的球員。

6 **much of the burden falls on** 大部分的負擔落在
bear the responsibility for 負起……的責任

Much of the burden for caring for the newborn has been on Sarah, as her husband often travels for work.
照顧新生兒的大部分重擔落在 Sarah 身上,因為她的丈夫經常需要出差。

As a team leader, **he bears the responsibility for ensuring** that every project is completed on time.
作為團隊的領導者,他負責確保專案可以如期完成。

7 **in a rush** 急於、匆忙
rush something through 匆忙完成某事
the last minute 趕在最後一刻

I was in a rush this morning and forgot to bring my wallet.
我今天早上太匆忙,結果忘了帶錢包。

He ended up making mistakes because **he was rushing through his homework** instead of taking his time.
他的作業有很多錯誤,因為他匆忙做完,而不是花時間仔細完成。

At **the last minute**, he found his passport.
他在最後一刻找到了他的護照。

TOPIC 8

Welcome to the Age of Avatars
虛擬分身時代來臨

虛擬分身。

元宇宙

擴增實境 AR
　　虛擬實境 VR

Reading

MP3 29

閱讀以下文章，粗體字部分是本文的關鍵短語，先想想它們的意思及用法，再跟著引導進行更多字彙擴充練習！

Turn on the TV, and there's a mouse trying to sell you something. Go into an Internet chatroom, and the people you chat with may be using monsters as avatars. **We're entering an age in which** characters of all kinds are **standing in for us**. Character culture is taking over – in business, online, and in the wonderful world of toys.

For decades, companies have used characters as mascots. Two famous ones are Tony the Tiger (from the USA) and the Michelin Man (from France). Thanks to modern technology, characters like these have grown into walking, talking spokespeople. **We've reached a point where** an animated pig "pitching" credit cards seems perfectly normal. Maybe it's because there are already too many ads featuring real people. Or it could be that we feel less pressure when a cute character tries to sell us something.

The growth of character culture is also seen in the way we represent ourselves on the Internet. When choosing avatars for Internet forums, chatrooms, and online games, few people use photos of themselves. They are more likely to use images of things they like and relate to, such as cartoon and movie characters. Interestingly, when we see a Snoopy or Mickey Mouse avatar, that becomes the way we imagine the person who is using it. Internet friends often comment that it's strange to meet in person. They're used to referring to each other by their online nicknames and imagining friends as their avatars. It's a good example of the "virtual" world becoming **just as important as** the "real world."

Connected to these trends is the growth of character toys. They're collected by adults as well as children. Popular ones include characters from comic books, cartoons, and video games. Then there are toys based on original characters created by artists. These "designer toys" are sold everywhere, from convenience stores to clothing shops. You can even have a toy of yourself made. Using several photographs, a specialty company can quickly turn you into a 3D figure!

We're becoming comfortable with the idea of listening to, speaking with, and even becoming characters. The next generation of online communities may **take this a step further**. Instead of 2D avatars, we may have 3D characters standing in for us. We're also likely to see more animals, monsters, and other animated figures selling us things. And, of course, there will always be new toys. As character culture grows, **the line between the real world and the virtual world will continue to blur**.

翻譯

打開電視，有一隻老鼠試圖向你推銷東西。進入網路聊天室，和你聊天的人可能用怪獸當作虛擬頭像。我們正進入一個「角色文化」當道的時代──不管是在商業、網路、還是玩具世界，角色無所不在，甚至取代了真人的地位。

幾十年來，各大公司一直使用角色作為吉祥物。其中兩個著名的例子是美國的 Tony the Tiger（東尼虎）和法國的米其林寶寶。隨著科技進步，這些吉祥物不再只是靜態的圖案，而是能走能說的代言人。現在，如果你看到一隻動畫小豬來推銷信用卡，似乎也變成一件稀鬆平常的事情。或許是因為廣告裡真人太多，看膩了；又或者，當一個可愛的角色推銷東西時，我們比較不會有壓力。

角色文化的發展，也反映於我們在網路上自我呈現的方式。當我們在論壇、聊天室或線上遊戲選擇頭像時，真正用自己照片的人反而很少。大多數人會選擇自己喜歡、覺得有共鳴的形象，例如卡通或電影角色。有趣的是，當我們看到史努比或米奇老鼠作為虛擬頭像時，我們往往會將其與使用者的形象聯想在一起。網友們常說，與線上朋友見面時會感覺很奇怪，因為他們早已習慣用網路暱稱稱呼彼此，並將朋友想像成他們的虛擬分身。這正是「虛擬世界」變得與「現實世界」同樣重要的一個好例子。

角色文化的興起，也帶動了角色玩具的熱潮，而且不只是小孩喜歡，連大人也瘋狂收藏。最受歡迎的，當然是漫畫、卡通和電玩角色。除此之外，還有藝術家專門設計的「設計師玩具」，甚至超商、服飾店都有販售。而現在，你甚至可以擁有「自己的」玩具──只要提供幾張照片，專門的公司就能幫你做出一個 3D 公仔！

我們越來越習慣與角色互動，甚至讓它們來代表自己。未來，網路社群可能會更進一步，不只是 2D 頭像，而是 3D 虛擬人物，讓我們用立體角色在虛擬世界中活動。同時，未來廣告中會出現更多動物或怪獸，甚至各種動畫角色來推銷產品。而角色玩具，也絕對會持續推陳出新。隨著角色文化的發展，現實與虛擬世界的界線，將變得越來越模糊。

The Age of Avatars

練習 A：用英文表達 Phrase in Action

用以下關鍵短語作為句子重點提示，試著用英文表達每一句話。不一定只有一種說法！

1　we're entering an age in which
如今我們來到這樣的時代，AI 開始能從表情和語氣中讀出我們的情緒。當然這些都還言之過早，但是這可能會徹底改變我們的未來。

📎 敘述發展階段：
1～3 這些短語用來指出變化的時間點，以及階段性的轉變。

2　we've reached a point where
如今，虛擬分身不再只是簡單的圖像照片而已，它們可以移動、說話，甚至表達情感。

3　the line between A and B will continue to blur
隨著網紅開始打造 AI 版的自己，真實和虛擬的界線只會越來越模糊。

📎 表達觀點與分析：
4～6 這些短語偏向評論與延伸討論，闡述某事的重要性與進一步思考的方向。

4　stand in for us
未來，AI 虛擬分身或許會在工作中代替我們處理簡單工作以及與人互動。

5　just as important as
在線上聊天時，掌握合適的語氣和不打錯字一樣重要。

6　take this a step further
我們可以再進一步想像一個未來，在那裡人們可以完全在虛擬世界中上學或工作。

The Age of Avatars

MP3 30

練習 B：記憶挑戰 Phrase Recall!

以下是練習A各句子的參考英文說法，但關鍵短語不見了！你還記得它的中文怎麼說嗎？

*Reference Only – Not the Only Way!

1（我們正進入……這樣的時代）
We're entering an age in which AI can sense how we feel based on our facial expressions and tone of voice. Although it's still early days, this could change everything.

2（　　　　　　　　　　　　　）
We've reached a point where avatars are more than just profile pictures. They can move, talk, and even express emotions.

3（　　　　　　　　　　　　　　　　）
Now that influencers are creating AI versions of themselves, the line between what's real and what's virtual will continue to blur.

4（　　　　　　　　　　　　　）
In the future, AI-powered avatars might stand in for us at work, handling simple tasks and interactions.

5（　　　　　　　　　　　　　）
Getting the tone right in a chat is just as important as avoiding typos.

6（　　　　　　　　　　　　　　　　）
We can take this a step further and imagine a future where people can attend school or work entirely in virtual reality.

TOPIC 8 虛擬分身時代來臨　95

Let's Chat!

練習 C：靈活應用 Phrase Remix!

同樣的短語，放進生活其他情境中應用看看！
你也可以試著造自己的句子！

1 we're entering an age in which
我們正進入一個比起親朋好友推薦，人們更信任網路評論的時代。

2 we've reached a point where
我們已經來到這樣的時代──即使是對好朋友，
傳訊息也比打電話來得自然。

3 the line between A and B is becoming blurred
要分辨真實還是偽造的影片變得越來越困難，真與假之間的界線
也越來越模糊。

4 stand in for
如果你需要點綠色來裝飾菜餚，可以用胡蘿蔔葉來取代香菜。

5 just as important as
在求職面試中，自信和經驗一樣重要。

6 take this a step further
讓我們更進一步探討這個想法，並考慮它如何應用於其他行業。

Let's Chat!

MP3 31

練習 D：記憶挑戰 **Phrase Recall!**

以下是練習 C 各句子的參考英文說法，但關鍵短語不見了，而且還變長了！試著用你的話來描述這些被標示的語言段！

*Reference Only – Not the Only Way!

1 (　　　　　　　　　　　　　　)
We're entering an age in which people trust online reviews more than personal recommendations.

2 (　　　　　　　　　　　　　　)
We've reached a point where texting feels more natural than calling, even with close friends.

3 (　　　　　　　　　　　　　　　)
It's getting harder to tell the difference between real and fake videos. The line between reality and deception is becoming blurred.

4 (　　　　　　　　　　　　　　)
Carrot tops can stand in for coriander when you need a nice green touch.

5 (　　　　　　　　　　　　　　　)
In job interviews, confidence is just as important as experience.

6 (　　　　　　　　　　　　　　　)
Let's take this idea a step further and consider how we could apply it to other industries.

TOPIC ❽ 虛擬分身時代來臨　97

Expand! （關鍵短語 1 + 1 > 2 !!） MP3 32

看看本單元學過的關鍵短語，還可以延伸出哪些相關說法呢？繼續擴充你的口說及寫作素材吧！

1
We're entering an age in which... 我們正進入一個……的時代
We're witnessing a shift... 我們正在見證……的轉變
It's becoming increasingly common. 現在這種情況越來越常見了。

More than ever, we find ourselves in a world where people are using AI tools to write, design, and brainstorm ideas. **It's becoming increasingly common**. Technology isn't just helping us at work; it's becoming part of our lives.
現在，比起過去任何時候，我們都更深刻地感受到──越來越多人開始使用 AI 工具來寫作、設計和發想點子，這已經變得非常普遍。科技不再只是幫助我們工作，它已經成為我們生活的一部分。

2
The line between A and B becomes blurred...
A 和 B 之間的界線變得模糊
blur the line/distinction/boundary between A and B
A 和 B 之間越來越難區分
It's harder than ever to tell A from B.
比以往任何時候都更難分辨 A 與 B。

The artist's new piece **blurs the line between reality and fantasy**.
這位藝術家的新作品模糊了現實與幻想之間的區別。

With the rise of AI-generated writing, **it's harder than ever to tell** whether an online article was written by a human or a chatbot.
隨著 AI 生成寫作的興起，要分辨網路文章是由人類還是聊天機器人撰寫的變得比以往任何時候都更困難。

③
we've reached a point where... 我們已經來到……的階段
It's no longer surprising that... ……已經不再令人驚訝

We've reached a point where people rely on AI for everything from writing emails to making art, and **it's no longer surprising that** AI-generated content is everywhere.
現在已經到了人們從寫郵件到創作藝術，凡事都依賴 AI 的地步，所以 AI 生成的內容隨處可見也已經不再令人驚訝了。

④
stand in for us 代替我們
take something over 接替、接管、接手
fill in for us 臨時頂替我們
step in when we can't 在我們無法做到時介入

In modern households, smart home devices can automatically adjust the lights and air conditioning. When we're busy, **they can temporarily fill in for us** by replying to messages automatically. They can also detect gas leaks and send alerts when we're not at home.
在現代家庭中，智慧家電可以自動調整燈光和空調，在我們忙碌時，它們能暫時頂替我們，自動幫我們回覆訊息，還能在我們不在家時偵測瓦斯外洩發出警報。

When the main speaker has a last-minute issue, **a teammate can step in** and give the presentation instead.
當主講人有突發狀況時，其他隊員可以接替他上場，完成簡報。

⑤
just as important as... 與……同樣重要
shouldn't be overlooked... 不應被忽視
deserves just as much attention as... 與……一樣值得關注

Mental health is just as important as physical health and **shouldn't be overlooked**. It **deserves just as much attention as** diet and sleep in maintaining overall well-being.
心理健康與身體健康同樣重要，不應被忽視。在維持健康這件事情上，它應該如同飲食、睡眠一樣受到重視。

6
take something a step further... 更進一步來看
look deeper into this... 深入探討這點……
If we take a closer look... 如果我們仔細看看、深入了解

Many people assume that social media only affects how we stay connected, **but if we look deeper into this**, we'll see that it also shapes our self-esteem, attention span, and even decision-making.
很多人以為社群媒體只影響我們如何跟他人保持聯繫，但如果我們深入探討，就會發現它還在不知不覺中影響著我們的自尊、注意力，甚至是決策判斷能力。

Reusable shopping bags seem like a great way to be more eco-friendly, **but if we take a closer look**, we'll see that making them also consumes a lot of resources. That's why using them responsibly is just as important as switching away from plastic.
使用環保購物袋看起來是個好選擇，但如果我們更仔細地想，就會發現製造這些袋子其實也需要消耗大量資源。這就是為什麼善用它們，和減少使用塑膠袋一樣重要。

TOPIC 9

How English Evolved
英語的演變

語言
隨著時間進化。

現代英文

網路英文

澳洲腔

Reading

MP3 33

閱讀以下文章，粗體字部分是本文的關鍵短語，先想想它們的意思及用法，再跟著引導進行更多字彙擴充練習！

One interesting thing about languages **is** the way **they change over time**. In English, everything from spelling to vocabulary to pronunciation has gone through major changes over the centuries. In fact, to a modern speaker, the English of 1,000 years ago looks and sounds like a foreign language!

The history of English dates back around 1,500 years. At that time, groups of Europeans invaded England, bringing their languages with them. These gradually developed into Old English. Later, in 1066, England was invaded by the Normans, who sailed there from France. This caused the language to go through an important shift, leading to what we now call Middle English. The language **underwent further shifts** over the next 500 years, eventually becoming Modern English.

Over the centuries, one of the most obvious areas of change has been with pronunciation. In Old English, for instance, people said "hus" and "mus." Now we say "house" and "mouse." With Modern English, there are also pronunciation differences in the USA, the UK, Australia, and elsewhere. When people who speak the same language live in places separated by great distances, the language undergoes rapid changes from place to place.

English spelling has also gone through interesting changes. For example, in Old English, people wrote "riht." A "g" was added in Middle English, making the spelling "right." Also, in the distant past, people did not always follow standards of spelling. In the 18th and 19th centuries, scholars like Noah Webster wrote dictionaries, helping make the spelling more consistent. However, different standards were decided on in England and the USA. Clear differences remain today, such as "color" vs. "colour."

Vocabulary changes happen even more quickly. English has grown by borrowing words from many languages, including French, Spanish, and Arabic, to name a few. New food terms are common additions. "Tofu" and "sushi" are now standard English words, and even "edamame" is listed in some dictionaries. **Then there is** slang, with terms entering and leaving the language every year. For example, 40 years ago, you often heard people say "groovy," meaning "great." These days, you rarely hear the word, **except** in old movies and TV shows.

Because English is spoken by so many people worldwide, it's an exciting time for the language. Just as American and British versions are always changing, so are versions spoken in Canada, Singapore, India, and elsewhere. At the same time, an entirely new version of English is appearing on the Internet, with its own slang and writing styles. In a way, learning English **is a never-ending process**, even for native speakers.

翻譯

語言的一個有趣之處在於它們隨著時間而變化的方式。在英文裡，從拼字、詞彙到發音，幾個世紀以來都經歷了巨大的變化。其實，對現代人來說，1000 年前的英文看起來、聽起來就像是完全不同的外語！

英文的歷史大約可以追溯到 1500 年前，當時來自歐洲的族群入侵英格蘭，並帶來他們的語言，這些語言逐漸發展成「古英文」。後來，1066 年，來自法國的「諾曼人」入侵英格蘭，導致語言發生重大變化，形成「中古英文」。接下來的 500 年，語言又經過了多次轉變，最後成為我們現在使用的「現代英文」。

在這些變化中，發音的變化最明顯。比如，在「古英文」時代，人們說 hus 和 mus，但現在我們則說 house 和 mouse。到了「現代英文」，不同地區的發音也產生了差異，美國、英國、澳洲等地的發音各不相同。當使用相同語言的人群分散到不同的地方，語言就會在各地快速演變。

英文的拼字方式也發生了許多有趣的變化。例如，在「古英文」裡，人們寫 riht，後來在「中古英文」時期，加上了字母 g，變成了 right。此外，在過去，人們並沒有固定的拼字標準。18 和 19 世紀時，學者如 Noah Webster 編寫了字典，讓拼字變得更一致。不過，英國和美國最終選擇了不同的拼字標準，因此今天我們還能看到像 color 與 colour 這類拼字上的差異。

詞彙的變化速度甚至比發音和拼字還快。英文經常從其他語言借詞，例如法文、西班牙文、阿拉伯文等等。尤其是食物名稱，常常會被納入英文詞彙，例如 tofu（豆腐）和 sushi（壽司）現在已經是標準的英文單字，甚至 edamame（毛豆）也出現在一些字典裡。此外，俚語也是一大變化來源，每年都有新詞加入，也有舊詞消失。例如 40 年前，人們常說 groovy 來表示「很棒」，但現在這個詞幾乎只會出現在舊電影或電視節目裡。

由於全球有這麼多人在使用英文，這個語言一直在快速變化。美式英文與英式英文不斷演變，加拿大、新加坡、印度等地的英文也在發展出自己的特色。同時，網路上甚至出現了一種全新的「網路英文」，擁有獨特的俚語和書寫風格。可以說，學習英文是一個永無止境的過程，連母語人士都一直在適應新的變化！

How English Evolved

練習 A：用英文表達 *Phrase in Action*

用以下關鍵短語作為句子重點提示，試著用英文表達每一句話。不一定只有一種說法！

1　one interesting thing about Sth is…
語言的一個有趣之處在於，語言會隨著人們、文化和社會環境的變化而改變。

2　Then there is
再來就是語氣的影響。有時候，比起你說了什麼，怎麼說反而更關鍵。

3　except
除了在經濟或政治因素成為阻礙的情況之外，學習第二語言能打開了解不同文化的大門。

> 1～3 的短語常用於引導新的話題或補充說明，使敘述更加清楚和完整。

4　they change over time
語言會隨著時間改變，不僅在詞彙上，甚至在語法、發音和意義上都有變化，反映出社會不斷變化的特性。

> 4～6 的短語適合用來描述事物如何隨著時間推移而變化，例如語言、文化、社會現象等。

5　undergo further shifts
語言學習曾經僅限於課本和教室。隨著數位產品的出現，它變得更加靈活。現在，隨著 AI 工具的發展，它又發生了更進一步的變化。

6　is a never-ending process
學習新語言是一個無止境的過程，總是有新鮮的事物等著我們去發現。

How English Evolved

MP3 34

練習 B：記憶挑戰 **Phrase Recall!**

以下是練習 A 各句子的參考英文說法，但關鍵短語不見了！你還記得它的中文怎麼說嗎？

*Reference Only – Not the Only Way!

1（語言的一個有趣之處是）
One interesting thing about languages is that they are constantly evolving. They change with the people, the culture, and the social environment.

2（　　　　　　　　）
Then there's the way tone plays a role. Sometimes what you say isn't as important as how you say it.

3（　　　　　　　　）
Learning a second language can open doors to new cultures, except in situations where economic or political factors get in the way.

4（　　　　　　　　　　）
They change over time, not just in vocabulary but also in grammar, pronunciation, and even meaning, reflecting the ever-changing nature of society.

5（　　　　　　　　　　　）
Language learning used to be limited to textbooks and classrooms. With digital devices, it became more flexible. Now, with AI tools, it has undergone further shifts.

6（　　　　　　　　　　　）
Learning a new language is a never-ending process. There's always something new to discover.

TOPIC 9 英語的演變　　105

Let's Chat!

練習 C：靈活應用 Phrase Remix!
同樣的短語，放進生活其他情境中應用看看！
你也可以試著造自己的句子！

1 one interesting thing about Sth is...
園藝迷人的地方之一，是植物會隨著季節變化而展現不同的樣貌。

2 Then there is
在溝通互動的過程中，我們會受到許多因素影響。而肢體語言則是其中之一，它往往比言語更有說服力。

3 except
除了幾位正在度假的團隊成員之外，所有人都被邀請參加會議。

4 they change over time
我們的習慣會隨著時間改變，二十多歲時喜歡的活動，到了三十或四十歲時可能就不再那麼感興趣了。

5 underwent further shifts
在合併後，公司在管理層上經歷了進一步的變動。

6 is a never-ending process
認識自己是個永無止境的過程。你在變，世界也在變，你對自己的理解也會跟著變。

Let's Chat!

MP3 35

練習 D：記憶挑戰 Phrase Recall!

以下是練習 C 各句子的參考英文說法，但關鍵短語不見了，而且還變長了！試著用你的話來描述這些被標示的語言段！
*Reference Only - Not the Only Way!

1（關於……有趣的地方在於）
One interesting thing about gardening is how plants thrive differently depending on the seasons.

2（　　　　　　　　）
When it comes to communication, many factors influence how we interact. Then there is the role of body language, which often speaks louder than words.

3（　　　　　　　　）
Everyone was invited to the meeting, except for a few team members who were on vacation.

4（　　　　　　　　）
Our habits change over time—the activities we enjoy doing in our twenties may not be the same in our thirties or forties.

5（　　　　　　　　）
After the merger, the company underwent further shifts (changes) in its management.

6（　　　　　　　　）
Figuring out who you are is a never ending process. You change, the world changes, and so does your understanding of yourself.

TOPIC 9 英語的演變　107

Expand!（關鍵短語 1 + 1 > 2 !!）   MP3 36

看看本單元學過的關鍵短語，還可以延伸出哪些相關說法呢？繼續擴充你的口說及寫作素材吧！

❶ one interesting thing about Sth is... 有趣的地方是
set sth/sb apart 使某事／某人與眾不同

What **sets her apart from the rest of the team** is her sensitivity, which allows her to understand what's not said and reach out before being asked.
她與團隊其他成員不同的地方在於，她總能敏銳地察覺到別人沒說出口的事，並且在對方還沒開口前就主動提供幫助。

One interesting thing about studying history is how you realize there's nothing new under the sun, and we always seem to repeat the same mistakes.
讀歷史的有趣之處之一就是，你會發現，天底下沒有新鮮事，我們總是重複著相同的錯誤。

❷ Then there is 還有
Don't forget about 也別忘了

When discussing ways to stay healthy, we talk about exercise and nutrition. **Then there's** mental health, which we often overlook.
當談到保持健康的方法時，我們會談到運動和營養。然後還有心理健康，這一點常常被我們輕忽了。

Don't forget about getting enough sleep. It's essential for our health and emotional well-being.
可別忘了還有充足的睡眠，它對我們的健康和幸福快樂非常重要。

except 除了
③ apart from 除了
leave someone/something out 除去、略過

She cleaned the whole house **except the kitchen**. **Apart from the dishes**, everything else was spotless. **She left out the kitchen** because she ran out of time.
她打掃了除了廚房以外的整間房子。除了碗盤，其他地方都非常乾淨。沒打掃廚房只是因為她沒時間了。

④ they change over time 隨著時間改變
as time passes 隨著時間過去

When you look at city landscapes, **they change over time**. (**As time passes**,) they begin to take on new forms with modern buildings replacing older ones.
當你看城市的風景時，它們會隨著時間而改變，新的現代建築逐漸取代老舊建築。

⑤ underwent further shifts 經歷了進一步的變化
keep evolving 繼續發展

The fashion industry **underwent further shifts** as online shopping became popular. It didn't stop changing; it **kept evolving**.
隨著網路購物興起，時尚產業經歷了進一步的變革，它並沒有停止改變，而是不斷進化。

6 **is a never-ending process** 是一個永無止境的過程
is an ongoing journey 是一段持續的旅程

You finish writing something. You stare at it, and you hate it. So you rewrite, you second-guess, you spiral. And when it's almost done, you start all over again. **It's a never ending process**.
你寫了一段文章,看著它,覺得自己寫的真差。於是你重寫、懷疑自己、陷入無限迴圈。等到它終於快完成了,你又從頭來過。這是一個永無止境的過程。

Writing isn't just about finishing something. **It's an ongoing journey**. The moment you place the last period, the story isn't over. It whispers to you and to the hearts of unknown readers.
寫作不僅僅是完成一件事,它是一段持續的旅程。當你寫下最後一個句點的那一刻,故事沒有結束。它在你和那些未曾遇見的讀者心中輕聲低語。

Art, Style & Culture

藝術、風格與文化

PART 3

TOPIC 10

Sotheby's: When the Hammer Falls

蘇富比：億萬落槌

蘇富比

萬物皆有其價。

稀世珍品

畫作

珠寶

Reading

MP3 37

閱讀以下文章，粗體字部分是本文的關鍵短語，先想想它們的意思及用法，再跟著引導進行更多字彙擴充練習！

As the saying goes, everything has its price. People looking to get top dollar for their rarest possessions often turn to Sotheby's, a leading auction house. For more than 270 years, Sotheby's has sold countless art treasures. Along the way, the storied company has been **no stranger to** controversy.

Sotheby's **traces its roots** to March 11, 1744. On that day, the company's founder, Samuel Baker, auctioned a collection of books for a client in London. Sotheby's went on to sell many paintings, jewels, and other rare goods. That includes historical documents like a copy of the Magna Carta and artistic masterpieces by Rembrandt and Picasso. Sotheby's now holds 250 auctions a year in Paris, London, and elsewhere. **With the rapid growth of** the Chinese art market, a location was opened in Beijing in 2012. Sometimes, auctions reach eye-opening prices. Edvard Munch's *The Scream* sold for a record $120 million in May 2012.

Despite this success, controversy in the art world is rarely far away. In April 2013, Sotheby's auctioned some artifacts from Central and South America. The governments of four countries said many of the works were stolen cultural treasures. Sotheby's disagreed, and the sale went ahead. Another case that year involved a 900-year-old work of Chinese calligraphy by Su Shi. Some scholars said the work was a fake. Sotheby's researched the piece, concluded that it was real, and let the $8.2 million sale stand.

Sotheby's has strong competition in the field, especially from French auction house Christie's. Both firms work hard to persuade collectors to sell key pieces. A single masterpiece can make an auction **a must-see event**, helping lift the prices of other works. Sotheby's is skilled at generating such interest, as it auctioned $5.1 billion worth of goods in 2013. **Not surprisingly**, several **records were broken** in the process. It will be exciting to watch more records crumble as the hammer falls at future Sotheby's auctions.

翻譯

俗話說：「萬物皆有其價。」對於那些想讓自己最珍貴的收藏品賣出最高價的人來說，蘇富比無疑是首選。作為全球頂尖的拍賣行，蘇富比已有 270 多年的歷史，期間售出了無數藝術珍品。然而，這家擁有輝煌歷史的公司，也從未遠離爭議。

蘇富比的故事始於 1744 年 3 月 11 日。那一天，創辦人塞繆爾・貝克在倫敦為客戶拍賣了一批書籍。此後，蘇富比的拍賣範圍逐步擴展，涵蓋畫作、珠寶及其他稀世珍品，其中包括《大憲章》這類重要歷史文件，以及林布蘭和畢卡索的藝術傑作。如今，蘇富比每年在巴黎、倫敦等地舉辦約 250 場拍賣會。隨著中國藝術市場的快速崛起，2012 年，蘇富比也在北京開設了拍賣據點。有時，拍賣價格高得驚人，比如在 2012 年 5 月，愛德華・孟克的經典畫作《吶喊》以破紀錄的 1.2 億美元成交。

然而，成功的背後總伴隨著爭議。2013 年 4 月，蘇富比拍賣了一批來自中南美洲的文物，但四個國家的政府指控其中許多是被盜的文化瑰寶。蘇富比不同意這一說法，最終拍賣仍如期進行。同年，另一場爭議涉及一幅據稱出自蘇軾之手的 900 年前書法作品。儘管有學者質疑其真偽，但蘇富比經過調查後認定為真品，最終以 820 萬美元成交。

蘇富比在這個領域面臨激烈競爭，尤其是來自法國拍賣行佳士得的挑戰。兩家公司都努力說服收藏家出售重要作品，因為一件重量級的藝術品，能讓整場拍賣會成為市場焦點，進而推高其他拍品的價格。蘇富比擅長營造這種關注度，2013 年的拍賣總額達到 51 億美元。在此過程中，數項紀錄被刷新也就不足為奇了。未來，隨著拍賣槌落下，更多紀錄的誕生將令人拭目以待。

PLUS! 主題實用詞彙精選

- Everything has its price.（Everything that you desire in life comes with a price.）凡事皆有代價。想得到什麼，就得付出相應的代價。
- auction house 拍賣行
- hammer price 落槌價（最終成交金額）
- the winning bidder 得標者
- buyer's premium 買家按成交價應付的佣金
- top dollar 最高價、（願意付出的）高價
- It was a fake. 那是贗品
- He was a fake. 他是冒牌貨

When the Hammer Falls

練習 A：用英文表達　Phrase in Action

用以下關鍵短語作為句子重點提示，試著用英文表達每一句話。不一定只有一種說法！

1 As the saying goes,
俗話說，「有錢萬能」，這一點在拍賣行中更為明顯。房間裡充滿了各種語言交談聲，而最終能得到稀世珍寶的人，是出價最高的人。

2 Not surprisingly
一條神祕的 18 世紀鑽石項鍊即將拍賣。毫不意外的，它與瑪麗安東尼皇后的關聯引起了大家的關注。

> 1～2 的短語用來表達習慣性或普遍的觀點。

3 With the rapid growth of
隨著數位平台的迅速發展，二級藝術市場變得更加容易接觸。

> 3～4 的短語可以用在：描述事物的起源，並接著講述隨著發展帶來的變化，形成一條簡單的敘事脈絡。

4 trace its roots
根據希臘歷史學家希羅多德的說法，拍賣傳統可追溯到古巴比倫，當時婦女被當作財產拍賣以作婚配。

5 be no stranger to something
藝術市場對於天價是一點也不陌生的。Picasso 的《阿爾及爾的女人》曾經以 1.6 億美元售出。

6 a must-see event
大型藝術博覽會和頂級拍賣會是收藏家尋找珍稀藝術品時不可錯過的盛事。

7 records were broken
沃荷的《坐牛》以 147,044 英鎊成交，打破了拍賣會上 37,800 英鎊的先前紀錄。

When the Hammer Falls

MP3 38

練習 B：記憶挑戰 Phrase Recall!

以下是練習 A 各句子的參考英文說法，但關鍵短語不見了！你還記得它的中文怎麼說嗎？

*Reference Only - Not the Only Way!

1 (　　　俗話說　　　)
As the saying goes, "Money talks," and it's easy to see how true that is at auction houses. The murmur of diverse languages fills the room, and in the end, the masterpiece will be sold to the highest bidder.

2 (　　　　　　　)
A mysterious 18th-century diamond necklace with possible links to Queen Marie Antoinette will be auctioned. Not surprisingly, its backstory has caught people's attention.

3 (　　　　　　　)
With the rapid growth of digital platforms, the secondary art market is now more accessible.

4 (　　　　　　　)
According to the Greek historian Herodotus, the tradition of auctions traces its roots to ancient Babylon, where women were sold for marriage.

5 (　　　　　　　)
The art market is no stranger to jaw-dropping prices. Picasso's *Les femmes d'Alger* once sold for 160 million dollars.

6 (　　　　　　　)
March Fine Art Auction 2025 is a must-see event for collectors seeking rare and valuable pieces.

7 (　　　　　　　)
Records were broken at the auction when Warhol's *Sitting Bull* sold for £147,044, surpassing the previous record of £37,800.

TOPIC ⑩ 蘇富比：億萬落槌

Let's Chat!

練習 C：靈活應用 Phrase Remix!
同樣的短語，放進生活其他情境中應用看看！
你也可以試著造自己的句子！

1 As the saying goes
俗話說，人生只有一次，所以我決定臨時訂機票飛去義大利。

2 Not surprisingly
毫不意外，他得到了晉升，他對待工作真的是盡心盡力。

3 With the rapid growth of
隨著社群媒體的快速成長，越來越多公司利用網紅行銷並在社群上廣告。

4 trace its roots
現代瑜伽可追溯至古印度，當時瑜伽是一種身心修行的方式。

5 be no stranger to something
在和不熟的人寒暄時，我對那種尷尬冷場的局面一點都不陌生啊。

6 a must-see event
跨年夜的年度煙火秀是當地人和遊客都不能錯過的盛事。

7 records were broken
當地這家麵包店的可頌，一天就賣出破紀錄的數量。

Let's Chat!

MP3 39

練習 D：記憶挑戰 Phrase Recall!

以下是練習C各句子的參考英文說法，但關鍵短語不見了，而且還變長了！試著用你的話來描述這些被標示的語言段！

*Reference Only – Not the Only Way!

1 (　　　　　　　　　　　)
As the saying goes, you only live once, so I decided to book that last-minute trip to Italy.

2 (　　　　　　　　　)
Not surprisingly, he got the promotion. He always went the extra mile.

3 (　　　　　　　　　　　)
With the rapid growth of social media, more companies leverage influencer marketing and run social media advertising campaigns.

4 (　　　　　　　　　　　)
Modern yoga traces its roots (back) to ancient India, where it was practiced for both mental and physical well-being.

5 (　　　　　　　　　　　)
I'm no stranger to awkward silences in small talk.

6 (　　　　　　　　)
The annual fireworks show on New Year's Eve is a must-see event for both locals and tourists.

7 (　　　　　　　　)
Records were broken at the local bakery when they sold more croissants in a day than ever before.

TOPIC ⑩ 蘇富比：億萬落槌　119

Expand! （關鍵短語 1 + 1 > 2 !!）　　MP3 40

看看本單元學過的關鍵短語，還可以延伸出哪些相關說法呢？繼續擴充你的口說及寫作素材吧！

❶
As the saying goes 俗話說
Like they always say 就像大家常說的
You know what they say 大家都這麼說

As the saying goes, breakfast is the most important meal of the day.
俗話說，早餐是一天中最重要的一餐。
= **Like they always say**, starting your morning right makes a huge difference.
就像大家常說的，一日之計在於晨。
= **You know what they say**, a good day begins with a good meal.
很多人都相信，一天的好壞取決於早餐吃得好不好。

❷
Not surprisingly 毫不意外
no wonder 難怪
of course 當然

Not surprisingly, the café was packed this morning. They just started selling their holiday special. **No wonder** everyone was talking about it. **Of course**, I had to try it too.
今天早上咖啡廳大排長龍，因為他們剛開始推出聖誕節限定的飲品。想也知道會這樣。難怪大家都在說這件事情。當然，我也一定要去買來喝喝看了。

❸
With the rapid growth of 隨著……的快速成長
With the increasing demand for 隨著對……需求的增加
as more and more people... 隨著越來越多人……

With the rapid growth of remote work, companies are rethinking how they use office space.
隨著遠端工作的快速成長，企業開始重新思考辦公空間的使用方式。

120

With the increasing demand for flexible schedules, many businesses are adopting hybrid work models **as more and more people prefer working from home**.
隨著對彈性工時的需求增加，許多公司開始採用混合辦公模式，因為越來越多人更喜歡在家工作。

> **4**   **trace its roots** 追溯……的起源
> **trace the origin of** 追溯……的起源
> **trace one's history (back) to** 其歷史可追溯到……

This festival **traces its roots to** a small local celebration. Neighbors would gather to share food and music.
這個節日最早只是當地人小規模的聚會，鄰居們會一起分享食物和音樂。

The University of Edinburgh **traces its history back to** 1583.
愛丁堡大學的歷史可以追溯到 1583 年。

> **5**   **be no stranger to something** 對……並不陌生
> **been through this before** 之前經歷過這樣的事情
> **know the drill** 知道規矩流程、知道該怎麼做

He's no stranger to intense workouts and **is completely used to** pushing himself to the limit at the gym.
他對高強度訓練並不陌生，也已經習慣了在健身房挑戰自己的極限。

I've been through this before, so I know exactly how stressful it is to run late for an interview because of traffic.
我之前也經歷過，所以我知道因為塞車而面試遲到有多令人崩潰。

You don't have to explain how to do it. We all **know the drill**. Don't worry.
你不需要解釋怎麼做，我們都知道流程，別擔心。

TOPIC **10** 蘇富比：億萬落槌   121

6
　a must-see event 不容錯過的盛事
　be the talk of the town 街頭巷尾都在討論的話題
　something you don't want to miss 你絕對不想錯過的

The championship game this weekend **is a must-see event**. Everyone's talking about it. Trust me, **it's something you don't want to miss**.
這週末的冠軍賽是<u>不容錯過的盛事</u>，<u>大家都在討論</u>。真的，<u>你絕對不想錯過這場比賽</u>。

7
　records were broken 紀錄被打破
　made history 創造了歷史

Many **records were broken** at the marathon this year.
今年的馬拉松中，許多<u>紀錄被刷新了</u>。

The team **made history** by winning the championship after 50 years.
這支隊伍時隔 50 年後再度贏得冠軍，<u>寫下歷史的一頁</u>。

TOPIC 11

Go Retro
復古風

復古風。

懷舊

時尚

喇叭褲

古著

波卡圓點印花

Reading

MP3 41

閱讀以下文章，粗體字部分是本文的關鍵短語，先想想它們的意思及用法，再跟著引導進行更多字彙擴充練習！

It might be time to look in your parents' closet for something to wear. Many styles from 20 or 30 years ago that went "out of fashion" for a while are now **back in vogue**. The surge in popularity of items with an "old school" feeling includes clothing, accessories, and much more. From "bell-bottom" jeans from the 1960s to sunglasses from the 1980s, **everything old is new again**!

The fashion cycle lasts around 20 years. A trend starts out red hot. Then it gets warm, cool, and then cold for 15-20 years. **That's how long it takes** for a new generation (who never went through the fad) to grow up and "rediscover" old fashions. At the same time, starting in their 30s, the people who originally went through the fad often **get nostalgic** for it. They may visit "vintage style" shops or websites to relive feelings from their past.

There are two ways for a person to go retro. The first is to buy actual vintage items. Stores, e-tailers, and auction sites sell just about **everything you can think of**. Need a pair of cowboy boots from the 1950s? No problem. A pair of sunglasses from the 1960s? Also easy. But be prepared for some **sticker shock**. High-demand items like vintage leather jackets and Levi's jeans can be very expensive. The other way to go retro is to look for new products using older designs and styles. For example, a retro style clock may be made to look like your grandfather's clock, but on the inside, it will contain 21th century technology. Some companies blend retro and modern styles. This has been done with great success by car makers like Volkswagen (with the Beetle) and BMW (with the Mini Cooper).

Fashion experts suggest being moderate when adding a retro flavor to your look. For example, an old polo shirt might **go great with** a new jacket. Accessories like vintage handbags and watches can also help you stand out. But overdoing it, the experts warn, **is a no-no**. Wearing an entire outfit from the 1970s, for example, may make you stand out more than you want to.

One thing's for certain – **there is no lack of** colors, patterns, or designs to choose from. The last 50 years have seen an explosion of new trends and styles. So if you're feeling bored with your look, check out an old clothing catalogue for inspiration. Or, **to liven up** your home or office, consider looking to the past for some great ideas.

翻譯

現在也許該去你父母的衣櫥裡找找看有什麼可以穿的衣服了。許多 20 或 30 年前一度「過時」的風格，現在又重新成為時尚潮流。那些帶有「復古」感覺的物品越來越受歡迎，包括服裝、配件等等。從 1960 年代的「喇叭褲」到 1980 年代的太陽眼鏡，所有曾經的「舊物」現在又成為新的時尚！

時尚的循環大約是 20 年。一個潮流剛開始非常熱門，接著慢慢變得不那麼流行，冷卻下來，然後沉寂個 15 到 20 年。這段時間足夠讓一個全新的世代（從未經歷過這股潮流）長大，並「重新發現」這些舊時尚。而同時，從 30 歲開始，最初經歷過那些潮流的人，往往也會對當年的流行產生懷舊情感。他們可能會去「復古風格」商店或網站，回味當時的感覺。

有兩種方式可以走復古風。第一種是購買真正的復古物品。各種商店、網路商家和拍賣網站幾乎什麼都賣。需要一雙 1950 年代的牛仔靴？沒問題。1960 年代的太陽眼鏡？也很容易找到。但要有心理準備，價格可能會讓你嚇一跳。像復古皮衣或 Levi's 牛仔褲這種高需求商品可能非常昂貴。另一種走復古風的方式是尋找使用舊有設計和風格的全新產品。例如，一款復古風時鐘外觀看起來像是你爺爺的時鐘，但內部卻搭載 21 世紀的科技。有些公司會把復古與現代風格結合。像 Volkswagen（福斯的金龜車）和 BMW (Mini Cooper) 等汽車製造商就成功地實現了這一點。

時尚專家建議，在穿搭中加入復古元素時要適度。例如，一件舊款 polo 衫搭配一件新外套可能就很有型。像復古手提包和手錶等配飾也能幫助你脫穎而出。但專家也提醒，過度使用復古風格是不可取的。像是穿著整套 1970 年代的服裝，可能會讓你變得過於顯眼，反而不自在。

有一件事是肯定的──現在有各式顏色、圖案和設計可選擇。過去 50 年來，新潮流與新風格層出不窮。因此，若對自己的穿著感到無聊，不妨翻翻舊的服裝型錄尋找靈感。或者，想為你的家或辦公室增添活力，不妨從過去汲取一些很棒的創意。

Go Retro!

練習 A：用英文表達 Phrase in Action

用以下關鍵短語作為句子重點提示，試著用英文表達每一句話。不一定只有一種說法！

1　It might be time to
也許是時候翻開你的衣櫃，拿出那些 70 年代的喇叭褲來穿了。

2　back in vogue
高腰牛仔褲現在又流行回來，說真的，是衣櫥裡必備基本款。

3　That's how long it takes
法蘭絨襯衫在 90 年代風靡一時，現在又流行回來了。流行就是這樣，兜兜轉轉又回到原點。

📎 1～5 這些短語用於描述事物隨時間變化、循環或發展的過程。

4　everything old is new again
從 A 字裙到波卡圓點，這些舊時尚元素，現在正流行。

5　get nostalgic
當我看到百褶裙的時候，總會忍不住回想起學生時代。

📎 6 跟 7 用來描述事物的多樣性、範圍或充足的選擇。

6　everything you can think of
古著店賣的東西，從舊皮夾克到1990 年代流行的厚底運動鞋，應有盡有。

7　there is no lack of
男士的復古時尚單品從不缺經典元素——高腰西裝褲、古巴領襯衫、麂皮樂福鞋和飛行員墨鏡，這些單品歷久不衰。

8　sticker shock
當看到那件復古皮夾克的價格時，我有被嚇到，但它真的值得。

9　is a no-no
70 年代的迪斯可亮片元素很有趣，但如果你從頭到腳都是亮片就太過頭了。

10　to liven up
你可以用條紋或印花西裝外套來為穿搭增添活力，再搭配一條寬鬆闊腿褲，輕鬆打造復古風格。

11　go great with
那件風衣非常適合搭配一雙踝靴。

Go Retro!

MP3 42

練習 B：記憶挑戰 Phrase Recall!

以下是練習 A 各句子的參考英文說法，但關鍵短語不見了！你還記得它的中文怎麼說嗎？

*Reference Only – Not the Only Way!

1 （　或許是時候要去　）
It might be time to go through your closet and pull out those bell-bottom jeans from the '70s.

2 （　　　　　　　　）
High-waisted jeans are now back in vogue, and honestly, they're a wardrobe essential.

3 （　　　　　　　　　　　）
Flannel shirts were all the rage in the '90s, and they're apparently coming back. That's how long it takes.

4 （　　　　　　　　）
From A-line skirts to polka dots, it's clear that everything old is new again.

5 （　　　　　　　　）
When I see pleated skirts, I can't help but get nostalgic for my school days.

6 （　　　　　　　　）
Vintage shops sell everything you can think of, from old leather jackets to chunky sneakers in the 1990s.

7 （　　　　　　　　　　）
There is no lack of timeless pieces in men's retro fashion. Items like high-waisted trousers, Cuban-collar shirts, suede loafers, and aviator sunglasses never go out of style.

8 （　　　　　　　　　）
I got sticker shock when I saw the price of a vintage leather jacket, but it's definitely worth it.

9 （　　　　　　　　　）
Wearing disco sequins from the '70s might be fun, but wearing them from head to toe is a no-no.

10 （　　　　　　　　　）
You can liven up your wardrobe with a striped or patterned blazer, paired with wide-leg trousers for an effortless vintage style.

11 （　　　　　　　　　）
That trench coat goes great with a pair of ankle boots.

Let's Chat!

練習 C：靈活應用 Phrase Remix!
同樣的短語，放進生活其他情境中應用看看！
你也可以試著造自己的句子！

1　It might be time to
或許是時候要重新思考我們對智慧型手機的依賴程度，也同時正視科技帶來的負面影響，像是資訊爆炸與數位倦怠。

2　now back in vogue
座機電話又流行起來了嗎？它們又酷又復古，就像卡式錄音帶一樣。

3　That's how long it takes
通常每天練習，大約需要兩個月的時間。要讓小狗學會「坐下」和「停留」這樣的基本指令，就是需要這麼久。

4　everything old is new again
90 年代的時尚又回來了，從短版上衣到寬褲，舊的東西再度流行起來。

5　get nostalgic
每次看到老式的翻蓋手機，我都會想到我們曾經有多在乎手機鈴聲這件事啊！

6　everything you can think of
這家店是購買居家必需品的好地方，店裡有你能想到的所有東西。

7　there is no lack of
在新創這個圈子裡，充滿了源源不絕的新點子。

8　sticker shock
我本來只想買一雙基本款的跑步鞋，結果看到標價時簡直嚇傻了。

9　is a no-no
開車時使用手機是絕對不可以的。

10　to liven up
用幾盆室內植物和暖色照明，就能讓沉悶的辦公空間增添一點生氣。

11　go great with
一張時尚的咖啡桌，可以讓新買的沙發更加亮眼。

128

Let's Chat!

MP3 43

練習 D：記憶挑戰 Phrase Recall!

以下是練習C各句子的參考英文說法，但關鍵短語不見了，而且還變長了！試著用你的話來描述這些被標示的語言段！

Reference Only – Not the Only Way!

1 (是時候去重新思考)
It might be time to reconsider how much we rely on smartphones and face the dark side of technology, including information overload and burnout.

2 (   )
Are landline phones back in vogue/style? They're cool and retro, just like cassette players.

3 (   )
It usually takes about two months of daily practice. That's how long it takes to train a dog to follow basic commands, like sit and stay.

4 (   )
The '90s are making a huge comeback in fashion. From crop tops to baggy pants, everything old is new again.

5 (   )
Every time I see an old flip phone, I get nostalgic for the days when ringtones were a big deal.

6 (   )
The store is the place to go for apartment essentials. It has everything you can think of.

7 (   )
There is no lack of innovative ideas in the startup community.

8 (   )
I wanted to buy a basic pair of running shoes, but when I saw the price, I had sticker shock.

9 (   )
Using your phone while driving is a definite no-no.

10 (   )
You can liven up a dull office space with some indoor plants and warm lighting.

11 (   )
A stylish coffee table can go great with the new sofa you bought.

TOPIC ⑪ 復古風   129

Expand! (關鍵短語 1 + 1 > 2 !!)   MP3 44

看看本單元學過的關鍵短語,還可以延伸出哪些相關說法呢?繼續擴充你的口說及寫作素材吧!

1
It might be time to 也許是時候
You might want to think about 你可能要好好想想

It might be time to think about the environmental impact of fast fashion, as it's adding to the problem of pollution and waste.
現在或許是開始思考快時尚對環境影響的最佳時機,因為它正在加劇污染和資源的浪費。

You might want to think about the link between child labor and the fashion industry, since cheap and unregulated child labor is still a major issue in the fashion industry.
你可能需要思考一下童工與時尚產業之間的關聯,因為廉價且未受規範的童工問題仍然是時尚產業的一大隱患。

2
That's how long it takes 這就是它需要花費的時間
This is the amount of time we need 這是我們所需要花費的時間

It often takes years of consistent practice and patience. **That's how long it takes** to master a new language.
學會一門語言,通常需要多年持續的練習和耐心。

This is the amount of time we need before English starts feeling like second nature.
這是我們所要花費的時間,才能讓英文變得像使用母語一樣自然。

get nostalgic 懷舊情感
③ the good old days 過去的美好時光
bring back those sweet memories 美好的回憶浮現

Every time I see an old photograph, **I get nostalgic for the good old days** when life was simpler. **It really brings back those sweet memories** of summer vacations with my friends.
每當我看到一張舊照片,就會想起那些舊時光,當時的生活是那麼單純。甜美的回憶浮現,那是我跟好友們一起度過的暑假時光。

everything you can think of 你能想到的所有東西
everything under the sun 一切可能的事情
④ all sorts of things 各種各樣的事情
whatever comes to mind 任何你能想到的事情
from A to Z 從頭到尾、徹底完全地

The fashion brand uses **everything you can think of** when it comes to recycled materials including plastic bottles and sneakers.
這個時尚品牌在回收材料的使用上應有盡有,包括寶特瓶和運動鞋。

We sat at the café for hours, **talking about everything under the sun**.
我們坐在那家咖啡店裡聊了好幾個小時,天南地北什麼都聊遍了。

The flea market had all sorts of things such as old furniture, vintage clothes, accessories, home decor, appliances, and antique treasures.
跳蚤市場裡有各式各樣的東西,像是舊家具、古著、配飾、家居擺飾、小家電,還有古董珍玩。

The brainstorming session covered **whatever came to mind**, from new product ideas to ways to improve customer service.
腦力激盪會議上,大家討論了任何能夠想到的事情,從新產品創意到改善客戶服務的方法。

The course will teach you how to start your own business, **from A to Z**, covering marketing, finance, and operations.
這堂課會從頭到尾教會你如何創業,包括行銷、財務和營運管理等各方面。

5 **sticker shock** 因為看到價格而感到震驚
The price is a real eye-opener 價格令人大開眼界

When I saw the price of the luxury watch, **I got sticker shock**. It was far more expensive than I expected.
當我看到那隻名錶的價格時,我被價格嚇歪了。它比我預期的還要貴好多。

I looked up the world's most expensive wines the other day, **and the price is a real eye-opener**.
我那天在看世界最貴紅酒排行榜,那個價格真的讓我大開眼界啊。

6 **go great with** 非常搭配
go hand in hand with... 與……非常搭配

This dress goes great with a pair of black heels. It's perfect for a night out.
這件洋裝跟黑色高跟鞋很搭。非常適合晚上出門裝扮。

A cup of tea goes hand in hand with a good book, especially on a rainy afternoon.
一杯茶與一本好書非常搭,尤其是在雨天的午後。

7 **is a no-no** 是絕對不要的
It's a big mistake 這真的是大錯特錯
It's totally unacceptable 這真的完全不可以

Being late for a meeting is a no-no.
開會遲到是絕對不可以的。

It's totally unacceptable to talk loudly in a library.
在圖書館大聲說話是絕對不行的。

It's a big mistake to procrastinate, as it only creates unnecessary stress.
拖延是個錯誤的決定，因為只會增加不必要的壓力。

8
no lack of 不缺乏
plenty of 有很多

There is no lack of entertainment in this city, with countless theaters, museums, and live music venues.
這座城市好玩的應有盡有，多劇院、博物館和現場音樂表演。

There's plenty of food at the party. No one will go hungry.
派對的食物準備非常豐富，沒有人會餓著的。

9
liven (something) up 給……增色、為……添彩
spice something up 使……更加生動有趣

To liven up the party, we decided to play some upbeat music.
為了增添派對氣氛，我們決定播放節奏感強的音樂。

Adding a little bit of lemon zest can really **spice up your dish**, bringing out the flavors.
加一點檸檬皮屑真的能讓這道菜更有風味，帶出更多的口感。

Here's how to **spice up your speech** with personal stories.
想讓你的演講更有趣？試著加入自己的故事！

Notes

TOPIC 12

Lost Arts: The Rise and Fall of Handicrafts
失落的藝術：手工藝的消逝與傳承

消失中的
傳統工藝。

失傳

木雕

手工紙

世代相傳

Reading

MP3 45

閱讀以下文章，粗體字部分是本文的關鍵短語，先想想它們的意思及用法，再跟著引導進行更多字彙擴充練習！

In the past, nearly everything was made by hand. Craftspeople made cups, chairs, and other items that were both useful and beautiful. **Over time**, machines and factories became the main producers of goods. **That has led to** the disappearance of some handicrafts. Fortunately, **many arts have been kept alive** through public interest and passionate supporters.

One lost art is the illuminated manuscript. Like all books in Europe up until 1450, illuminated manuscripts were made by hand. The words were first copied onto a page. Artisans then added beautiful borders and illustrations. The first letter of a chapter was often made especially large and colorful. Paints made from natural materials provided the color, and thin strips of gold (called gold leaf) helped bring the design to life. However, creating these treasures was expensive and time-consuming. After the printing press was invented, fewer and fewer were made.

A more recent art form **lost to** technology is the hand-painted theater poster. In the mid to late 20th century, going to the movies in Taiwan, Japan, and elsewhere had a special touch. Outside theaters, moviegoers could see large paintings advertising the newest films. To make a billboard painting, an artist started with a small movie poster. From that, he or she painted a much larger version. The billboards emphasized the main actors and actresses, whose names were painted in large letters. After just a few decades, though, this art form was replaced by large posters made with modern printing methods.

But all is not lost. People in many countries are still interested in handicrafts. They pick up skills by attending classes and reading books, magazines, and websites. This has helped preserve arts such as pottery and jewelry making. At arts and crafts shows, craftspeople sell their goods and chat with shoppers, just as they did 1,000 years ago. Governments are also helping. For example, the Crafts Council of India helps craftspeople find new selling opportunities. Many of them meet up once a year at the Kamala Show to share ideas and sell their goods.

Modern technology has influenced our lives in many positive ways. Yet people still appreciate the personal touch of a handmade good. Making and buying traditional crafts are excellent ways to celebrate one's culture and keep it alive. **It's a shame that** not all lost arts can be brought back. But even when they **die out**, museums give us a chance to appreciate the care and effort that **went into** them.

翻譯

在過去，幾乎所有物品都是手工製作的。工匠們製作杯子、椅子等既實用又美觀的物品。隨著時間推移，機器和工廠成為主要的商品生產者，導致一些手工藝逐漸消失。幸運的是，許多藝術因公眾的興趣和熱情的支持者而得以保存下來。

其中一種失傳的藝術是泥金裝飾手抄本。和 1450 年以前歐洲所有的書籍一樣，泥金裝飾手抄本是完全手工製作的。工匠先將文字謄寫到紙上，然後再添加華麗的邊框和插圖。每個章節的第一個字母通常特別放大並塗上鮮豔的色彩。當時的顏料來自天然材料，而金箔則使設計更顯生動。然而，製作這些珍品既昂貴又耗時。印刷術發明後，這項工藝便逐漸式微。

另一種較近代、因科技發展而消失的藝術形式是手繪電影海報。在 20 世紀中後期，台灣、日本等地的觀眾在戲院門口可看到巨幅的電影手繪廣告，為觀影體驗增添獨特魅力。要製作這類廣告看板，藝術家會先參考小型電影海報再繪製成放大版。這些看板通常強調主要演員，並將他們的名字以醒目的大字呈現。然而，僅僅幾十年後，這項藝術便被用現代印刷方法製作的大型海報所取代。

但並非所有傳統工藝都已失落。許多國家仍對手工藝抱有濃厚興趣。人們透過參加課程、閱讀書籍、雜誌或瀏覽網站來學習這些技藝，這有助於保存陶藝、珠寶製作等傳統藝術。在工藝展覽上，工匠們販售自己的作品，並與顧客交流，就像千年前一樣。各國政府也在努力推廣傳統工藝。例如，印度工藝委員會協助工匠尋找新的銷售機會，許多工匠每年都會參加 Kamala Show，在此交流想法並銷售作品。

現代科技確實為生活帶來許多便利，但人們依然珍視手工製品的獨特溫度。創作和購買傳統工藝品不僅讓文化得以傳承，也是一種致敬歷史的方式。雖然有些失傳的藝術難以復興，但博物館仍讓我們得以欣賞這些藝術品背後的精湛技藝與匠心。

Handicrafts

練習 A：用英文表達 Phrase in Action

用以下關鍵短語作為句子重點提示，試著用英文表達每一句話。不一定只有一種說法！

1 over time
隨著時間過去，許多傳統工藝，如金銀線刺繡和手工紙，已經變得越來越罕見。

2 lost to
許多傳統的染色手工藝都已經被合成染料取代。

3 die out
傳統手工藝會消失嗎？透過資源支持和知識傳承，這些技藝仍有機會被保存下來。

> 1～3 的短語用於鋪陳某個現象隨時間的變化、演進、衰退或消失，適合用於背景說明與邏輯銜接。

> 4～6 的短語用於寫作中加入評論色彩與情感修辭，讓論述更加生動。

4 lead to
從精緻的唐卡畫到手工織作的帕什米納披肩，拉達克 (Ladakh) 的工藝反映了其豐富的文化遺產。不幸的是，現代化使得這些藝術形式逐漸式微。

5 but all is not lost
手工藝逐漸式微，但還有一線生機。新一代的藝術家正在振興傳統手工藝。

6 It's a shame that
很可惜，越來越少人有興趣去學習這些工藝。

7 keep alive
工坊和學徒制有助於維持傳統工藝的存續。

8 go into
製作這張手工地毯花費了很多心血。

Handicrafts

MP3 46

練習 B：記憶挑戰 Phrase Recall!

以下是練習A各句子的參考英文說法，但關鍵短語不見了！你還記得它的中文怎麼說嗎？

Reference Only – Not the Only Way!

1 (　隨著時間過去　)
Over time, many traditional crafts like gold-thread embroidery (goldwork) and handmade paper have become harder to find.

2 (　　　　　　　　)
Many traditional dyeing techniques have been lost to synthetic alternatives.

3 (　　　　　　　　)
Are traditional crafts dying out? Through education and support, they can still be preserved.

4 (　　　　　　　　)
From intricate Thangka paintings to Pashmina shawls, Ladakh's craftsmanship reflects its rich cultural heritage. Unfortunately, modernization has led to the decline of the art forms.

5 (　　　　　　　　)
Handmade crafts are fading away, but all is not lost. A new generation of artists is restoring them.

6 (　　　　　　　　)
It's a shame that fewer and fewer people are interested in learning these crafts.

7 (　　　　　　　　)
Workshops and apprenticeships help keep traditional crafts alive.

8 (　　　　　　　　)
A lot of effort went into making this handmade rug.

TOPIC ⑫ 失落的藝術　139

Let's Chat!

練習 C：靈活應用 Phrase Remix!
同樣的短語，放進生活其他情境中應用看看！
你也可以試著造自己的句子！

1 over time
隨著時間過去，廢棄的建築逐漸融入大自然的懷抱，藤蔓爬滿牆壁。

2 lost to
手寫信並沒有被電子郵件和簡訊取代，因為它們能表達出數位溝通無法呈現的個人情感。

3 die out
某些語言正逐漸消失，因為使用那個語言溝通的人口越來越少。

4 lead to
忽視水管漏水的小問題，可能會導致後續房屋結構嚴重損壞。

5 but all is not lost
暴風雨毀了大部分農作物，但還不算全盤皆輸，因為還有一些田地倖免於難。

6 It's a shame that
真可惜，這幾年有那麼多獨立書店關門歇業。

7 keep alive
講述家族故事可以讓傳統世世代代延續下去。

8 go into
這項新技術的研發花費了大量研究資源。

Let's Chat!

MP3 47

練習 D：記憶挑戰 Phrase Recall!

以下是練習 C 各句子的參考英文說法，但關鍵短語不見了，而且還變長了！試著用你的話來描述這些被標示的語言段！

Reference Only – Not the Only Way!

1 (　　　　　　　　　　)
Over time, abandoned buildings are reclaimed by nature, with vines creeping over walls.

2 (　　　　　　　　　　)
Handwritten letters aren't lost to emails and texts, as they add a personal touch that digital communication can't match.

3 (　　　　　　　　　　)
Some languages are dying out because fewer and fewer people speak them.

4 (　　　　　　　　　　)
Ignoring small plumbing problems can lead to serious structural damage.

5 (　　　　　　　　　　)
The storm ruined most of the crops, but all is not lost. Some fields were spared.

6 (　　　　　　　　　　)
It's a shame that so many independent bookstores closed in recent years.

7 (　　　　　　　　　　)
Telling family stories helps keep traditions alive for future generations.

8 (　　　　　　　　　　)
A lot of research went into developing this new technology.

TOPIC ⑫ 失落的藝術

Expand! (關鍵短語 1 + 1 > 2 !!)　　MP3 48

看看本單元學過的關鍵短語，還可以延伸出哪些相關說法呢？繼續擴充你的口說及寫作素材吧！

> **over time** 隨著時間的推移
> **as time goes by** 隨著時間流逝
> ❶ **in the long run** 長遠來看
> **little by little** 一步步地
> **with time** 隨著時間一天一天過去

A: Everyone says that **the pain you feel will fade away as time goes by**. It's been two years. What's wrong with me? Why does it feel like the pain will never go away?
大家都說，<u>隨著時間過去，痛苦會慢慢消失不見</u>。可是現在兩年都過去了，怎麼感覺這種痛苦永遠都不會消失。我到底為什麼會這樣。

B: It's okay to still feel this way. You have to tell yourself that.
你現在這樣的感覺沒有什麼不對，你要告訴自己這一點。

A: Anything can remind me of her. I hate it so much. Sometimes I even wish I had never met her.
我真的好討厭這樣，任何事情都可以讓我想到她，我甚至想過，要是我從來都沒有遇見過她該有多好。

B: Don't say that.
不要這樣想啦。

A: I know. Things will start making sense again **with time**. Healing **reveals itself little by little, blah, blah, blah**. I know these are all true, and I know you care about me. But now, it's just not yet. I can't.
我知道，<u>隨著時間慢慢過去</u>，這一切就會說得通了，<u>什麼療傷是一點一滴地</u>諸如此類的心靈雞湯，我都知道，我相信這都是真的，我也知道你很關心我。但現在，我還做不到，我真做不到。

❷ lost to 被……奪去、取代
swallow 吞噬

The "concrete river" has **swallowed** the quiet little village.
「都市發展的洪流」吞噬了那個寧靜的小村莊。

die out 滅絕、消失
❸ fade away 逐漸消失
erase 抹滅、清除

Dial-up internet **has pretty much died out in most places**.
大多數地區幾乎都沒有撥接上網了。

Over time, the pain of losing him **began to fade away**.
隨著時間推移,失去他的痛苦開始慢慢消退。

Their names were erased from the records as if they had never been there.
他們的名字從記錄中被抹去,就好像他們從未存在過一樣。

All is not lost. 仍有一絲希望
❹ There's still hope. 仍然有希望
It's not over yet. 還沒到最後呢

The situation looks bad, **but all is not lost**.
情況現在看來很糟糕,但是還不到大勢已去的地步。

Even when it seems impossible, **there's still hope**.
即使事情看似不可能,總還有希望的。

We are struggling now, **but it's not over yet**.
我們現在陷入膠著,但是還沒到最後一刻都不算輸。

TOPIC ⑫ 失落的藝術　143

5
lead to 導致
open the door to 為某事創造機會（開啓通往……的大門）
set the stage for 為某事創造有利條件／鋪路／打基礎
at a cost 以……為代價

A: I still can't believe that I just quit. And that's it. Wait, what if I made a mistake?
我還不敢相信我就這樣辭職了，然後就這樣了。等一下，會不會我根本就不該辭職？

B: Hey, don't overthink it. I think **it opens the door to new opportunities**.
我覺得現在有很多新的機會等著你啊，你不要過度憂慮了。

A: You're right. But I haven't seen any door, except the door to my anxiety.
希望就像你說的。但到目前為止，除了通往焦慮的那扇門之外，我什麼門都沒看到。

B: Oh, I'm sorry. I know it's a cliché to say **challenges set the stage for something better**, especially when what you're going through feels like the total opposite.
「挑戰是為更好的未來鋪路」這句話的確是陳腔濫調，尤其是當你正在經歷的感覺恰恰相反時。

A: I try to work on my mindset. I have freedom and all the possibilities, but **at a cost**.
我嘗試調整自己的心態。我現在擁有自由和無限的可能性，但這是有代價的。

6
It's a shame that 真可惜
if only things were different 要是情況不同就好了
a bitter pill to swallow 難以接受的殘酷事實

If only things were different, we wouldn't have to say goodbye.
要是情況不同就好了，我們就不必說再見了。

Losing the championship was **a bitter pill to swallow**.
輸掉冠軍賽是難以接受的殘酷事實。

7 **go into something**
(時間、金錢、精力等) 花在……上、開始從事某行業、開始進入某狀態
pour something into something
投入（大量心力、金錢、時間等）在……上

Many people **go into teaching** because they love working with kids.
有很多人<u>投身教育</u>的原因是喜歡跟孩子們相處。

The designer poured all his time and energy into the project.
<u>那位設計師全心全意投入</u>這個專案。

Notes

Cities & Tourism
城市與旅遊

PART 4

TOPIC 13

Adventure Tourism
冒險旅遊

冒險王
挑戰沒有極限。

世界最高峰

逛街購物我不要

Reading

MP3 49

閱讀以下文章，粗體字部分是本文的關鍵短語，先想想它們的意思及用法，再跟著引導進行更多字彙擴充練習！

While on vacation, not everyone likes staying at nice hotels, visiting museums, or shopping at department stores. Some would rather jump out of an airplane, speed down a river, or stay in a traditional village. They're part of a growing number of people who enjoy adventure tourism. It's a style of travel for people looking to **get more out of their vacations**.

With the Internet, **it's easier than ever to set up an adventure tour**. People can plan trips themselves, or they can find a suitable tour company online. Some popular countries to visit are Costa Rica, India, New Zealand, and Botswana. Their natural settings **make them perfect for outdoor activities** like hiking and diving. **Rich in** wildlife, they're also great for bird watching and safaris.

Learning about the local history and culture is also popular with adventure travelers. In Peru, people love visiting the ruins of Machu Picchu. Travelers in Tanzania enjoy meeting local tribes. In some countries, **it's even possible to live and work** in a village during a vacation. While building houses and helping research teams, travelers can enjoy local food and learn about the culture.

There are adventure tours for people of every age and experience level. Trips may include walking in beautiful valleys or climbing the world's tallest mountains. **Some tours are designed for women**, and others **have families in mind**. During easy trips, tourists may do everything on their own. On more difficult trips, like hiking in the Himalayas, they can hire guides.

Besides being a lot of fun, these trips mean big money for local economies. The global tourism sector is worth some $4 trillion. Of that, adventure tourism **makes up 26% of the market**, with around 150 million overseas trips taken yearly. **That number is growing** as more people are planning exciting, memorable vacations.

翻譯

在度假時，並不是每個人都喜歡住高級飯店、逛博物館或血拚購物。有些人更愛從飛機上一躍而下、沿著河流急速漂流，或住進當地的傳統村落。他們屬於那群越來越多的「冒險旅遊」愛好者，這是一種專為想讓旅程更刺激、更有挑戰性的人設計的旅遊方式。

有了網路，要安排一趟冒險之旅比以往更加簡單。人們可以自己規劃行程，也可以在網路上找到合適的旅遊公司。一些受歡迎的旅遊國家包括哥斯大黎加、印度、紐西蘭和波札那。這些國家擁有得天獨厚的自然環境，非常適合健行和潛水等戶外活動。由於野生動物資源豐富，也很適合賞鳥和參加狩獵旅行。

對冒險旅遊愛好者來說，探索當地的歷史與文化也是重點之一。像是在秘魯，遊客喜歡參觀馬丘比丘遺址；在坦尚尼亞，人們則會與當地部落互動。有些國家甚至提供機會，讓遊客在旅途中體驗當地生活，例如幫忙蓋房子或參與科學研究，邊做邊深入了解當地文化。

無論年齡與經驗，每個人都能找到適合的冒險行程。有些人喜歡漫步於風景秀麗的山谷，而有些人則選擇挑戰世界最高峰。某些行程專為女性設計，另一些則適合家庭旅遊。簡單的旅程，遊客可以自行探索；但如果是像攀登喜馬拉雅山這樣的高難度挑戰，就會需要專業嚮導協助。

除了帶來樂趣，冒險旅遊更是當地經濟的一大商機。全球旅遊業每年產值高達 4 兆美元，其中冒險旅遊占了 26%，每年約 1.5 億次海外旅遊選擇此類行程。隨著越來越多人嚮往刺激難忘的旅程，這個市場還會持續成長。

PLUS! 主題實用詞彙精選

- ☐ for people of every age 適合各個年齡層的人、老少皆宜
- ☐ a beginner / a first-timer 新手、第一次嘗試、無經驗的人
- ☐ rich in wildlife 野生動植物種類繁多
- ☐ the ruins of Machu Picchu 馬丘比丘遺跡
- ☐ local tribes 當地部落
- ☐ do everything on their own 一手包辦所有事情

Adventure Tourism

練習 A：用英文表達　Phrase in Action

用以下關鍵短語作為句子重點提示，試著用英文表達每一句話。不一定只有一種說法！

1 get more out of
當你離開海岸線、深入內陸時，你會更深刻地體會突尼西亞的魅力。在那些偏遠地區，你會發現悠久的傳統、通往撒哈拉沙漠的入口，以及古老的遺跡。

2 it's easier than ever
現在，透過各種旅行 App 和數位工具，計劃冒險旅行變得超簡單。我們可以輕鬆訂機票、找到價格實惠的 Airbnb 住宿，還能在網路上找到即時旅途資訊。

📎 1～7 這些短語都可以用來強調某個地方或是活動的特色。

3 make them perfect for
深藍色的高山湖泊和綠油油的阿爾卑斯山上草原，讓瑞士溫根成為戶外愛好者的天堂。

4 rich in
這裡的戶外活動非常豐富，從激流泛舟到高空滑索應有盡有。

5 it's even possible to
柬埔寨的奇帕村（Chi Phat）提供獨特的生態之旅。你甚至可以住在當地家庭，體驗他們的日常生活。

6 are designed for
有些旅遊方案專門針對數位遊牧族設計，提供長期住宿和彈性的工作環境。

7 have something in mind
有些飯店專為商務旅客打造，也有一些飯店會把焦點放在蜜月行程。

8 makes up
美食旅遊已成為觀光產業的重要一環，越來越多人為了吃而決定去哪旅行。

9 the number is growing
越來越多人想要獨特的旅行體驗，而且這個趨勢還在成長中。

📎 短語 8～9 常用於描述市場的趨勢與發展情形。

Adventure Tourism

MP3 50

練習 B：記憶挑戰 Phrase Recall!

以下是練習 A 各句子的參考英文說法，但關鍵短語不見了！你還記得它的中文怎麼說嗎？

*Reference Only – Not the Only Way!

1（想在旅途中獲得更多收穫）
You get more out of Tunisia when you step away from the coastline and explore the inland areas. In more remote places, you'll find age-old traditions, the gates of the Sahara and ancient ruins.

2（　　　　　　　）
It's easier than ever to plan an adventure trip, thanks to all the travel apps and digital tools. We can easily book flights, find affordable Airbnb places to stay, and get real-time tips online.

3（　　　　　　　　　　　）
Wengen, Switzerland, is known for its deep blue mountain lakes and lush green Alpine meadows. These features make it perfect for outdoor lovers.

4（　　　　　　）
This region is rich in outdoor activities, from white-water rafting to zip-lining.

5（　　　　　　　　　　）
Chi Phat in Cambodia offers a unique eco-trip. It's even possible to stay with local families and experience their daily lives.

6（　　　　　　　　　）
Some travel programs are designed for digital nomads, offering long-term stays and flexible work-friendly environments.

7（　　　　　　　　　）
Certain hotels cater to business travelers, while others have honeymooners in mind.

8（　　　　　　　）
Food tourism now makes up a major part of the travel industry, as more people plan their trips around what they eat.

9（　　　　　　　　　　）
More people want unique travel experiences, and the number is growing.

TOPIC 13 冒險旅遊   153

Let's Chat!

練習 C：靈活應用 Phrase Remix!
同樣的短語，放進生活其他情境中應用看看！
你也可以試著造自己的句子！

1 get more out of
如果你事先規劃，而不是一直滑手機，你的週末會過得更充實。

2 it's easier than ever
有了網路食品雜貨配送，冰箱補貨變得超簡單。

3 make it perfect for
這間公寓配有全套家具，包括廚房用品和寢具，非常適合短期住宿。

4 rich in
黑巧克力富含抗氧化劑，對健康有好處。

5 it's even possible to
有了 AI 工具，現在甚至只要輸入描述，就能生成畫作、圖片，甚至雕塑作品。

6 are designed for
降噪耳機專為需要在吵雜環境中集中注意力的人設計。

7 have something in mind
她每次做重大決定時，心裡都會考慮未來的職涯發展。

8 make up
現在自由工作者在整體勞動市場中占了很大比例。

9 the number is growing
隨著環保意識提升，電動車的數量也同時在增加。

Let's Chat!

MP3 51

練習 D：記憶挑戰 Phrase Recall!

以下是練習C各句子的參考英文說法，但關鍵短語不見了，而且還變長了！試著用你的話來描述這些被標示的語言段！
*Reference Only – Not the Only Way!

1 (   )
You'll get more out of your weekends if you plan ahead instead of just scrolling on your phone.

2 (   )
With online grocery delivery, stocking your fridge is easier than ever.

3 (   )
The apartment is fully furnished, with everything from kitchenware to bedding. That makes it perfect for short-term stays.

4 (   )
Dark chocolate is rich in antioxidants, which are good for your health.

5 (   )
With AI tools, it's even possible to generate paintings, images and even sculptures just by typing a description.

6 (   )
Noise-canceling headphones are designed for people who need to focus in noisy environments.

7 (   )
She has her future career in mind whenever she makes a big decision.

8 (   )
Freelancers now make up a large part of the workforce.

9 (   )
The number of electric cars on the road is growing as more people go green.

TOPIC ⑬ 冒險旅遊   155

Expand! （關鍵短語 1 + 1 > 2 !!） MP3 52

看看本單元學過的關鍵短語，還可以延伸出哪些相關說法呢？繼續擴充你的口說及寫作素材吧！

1
get more out of 更充分地利用、獲得更多
make the most of 好好利用

If you really want to **get more out of your trip**, you need to **make the most of your time**. Wake up early, explore beyond the tourist spots, and talk to locals. That way, you can maximize your experience. But remember, don't overdo it. Travel is meant to be relaxing.

如果你真的想讓這趟旅行<u>更有收穫</u>，你需要<u>好好利用時間</u>——早起、走出觀光區，並與當地人交流。這樣你才能玩得盡興。不過，還是剛好就好，旅行應該是要能放鬆享受的。

2
it's easier than ever 從來沒有像現在這麼容易
It's a breeze. 非常輕鬆容易。
It couldn't be simpler. 再簡單不過了。

With design platforms like Canva, creating graphics **is easier than ever**. **It's a total breeze**. You just pick a template, tweak a few details, and you're done. Honestly, **it couldn't be simpler!**

有了像 Canva 這樣的設計平台，設計圖像<u>從來沒有像現在這麼容易</u>。<u>非常簡單</u>，你只要選個模板、微調一點細節就搞定了。<u>真的再簡單不過了！</u>

3
rich in 富含
abundant 大量、充足、豐富的

The city **is rich in history and culture**.
這座城市<u>充滿歷史與文化氣息</u>。

The Amazon rainforest's **abundant rainfall** helps its ecosystems thrive.
亞馬遜雨林<u>豐沛的降雨量</u>讓這裡的生態系統可以生機蓬勃。

make them perfect for 讓它們特別適合……
4. It's just what you need 正是你所需要的
You couldn't ask for a better... 這是最好的……了

The warm weather and beautiful beaches **make this island perfect for a summer getaway**. Need a break from the hustle and bustle? **This island is just what you need**. The fresh seafood and friendly locals make the time you stay more enjoyable. No wonder it's been voted the most popular vacation spot three years in a row. **You couldn't ask for a better place** to spend your holiday.

溫暖的氣候和美麗的海灘，讓這座島成為完美的夏日度假勝地。想要遠離塵囂嗎？這裡非常適合你，新鮮的海鮮和熱情的當地人，讓你度假的每一刻都加倍愉快。難怪它連續三年被評為最受歡迎的度假勝地，這裡真的再適合度假不過了！

it's even possible to 甚至可以……
Believe it or not, you can... 你可能不敢相信，但你真的可以……
5. Would you believe that you can...? 你能想像居然可以……嗎？
It might surprise you, but you can...
你可能會不敢相信，但是你真的可以……

Believe it or not, you can fall asleep faster by putting your phone away an hour before bed.
你可能不敢相信，但睡前一小時不碰手機，你會更快入睡。

Would you believe that you can actually cook a decent meal in under 10 minutes?
你能想像嗎？其實不到 10 分鐘你就能做出一頓像樣的飯。

It might surprise you, but you can make your sneakers look brand new just by using toothpaste.
你可能會不敢相信，但只要用牙膏就能讓你的運動鞋看起來跟新的一樣。

6   **be designed for** 專為……設計
　　come with everything you need for... 自帶一切所需，適合……
　　you never have to worry about... 確保你再也不用擔心……

This travel-friendly coffee maker **is designed for coffee lovers on the go**. **It comes with everything you need for** a fresh cup of coffee anytime, and gives you the freedom to make coffee wherever you are. If you're someone who knows their coffee and has high standards, **you never have to worry about** settling for a cup that doesn't meet your expectations.
這台隨身咖啡機就是為了愛喝咖啡又常出門的人設計的。該有的配備全都有，讓你隨時隨地都能自己沖一杯咖啡。而且，如果你是對咖啡很講究、標準很高的人，以後出門再也不用擔心喝不到合你口味的咖啡了！

7   **with something in mind** 考慮到……
　　is shaped by... 受……影響而形成、由……塑造

This language-learning app was made to suit the needs of busy professionals. **Its structure is shaped by real-world conversations**, making lessons practical and easy to apply. Whether you're traveling or working abroad, you can tell it was developed **with real-life communication in mind**.
這款語言學習 App 是專門為了忙碌的專業人士所設計。它的課程設計都是運用真實對話，讓學習內容更實用。不管是旅行還是出國工作，你都能感覺到它的設計是圍繞真實溝通需求打造的。

8   **makes up** 構成、占比、是……的重要部分
　　account for 占……比例、是……的重要部分

Freelance work **makes up a big part of my income, accounting for nearly 60% of** what I earn each month.
接案子是我收入的一大部分，幾乎占了我每個月收入的 60%。

TOPIC 14

New York
紐約

紐約魅力。

曼哈頓

移民　大蘋果

聯合國總部

Reading

MP3 53

閱讀以下文章，粗體字部分是本文的關鍵短語，先想想它們的意思及用法，再跟著引導進行更多字彙擴充練習！

New York City has a special personality. It's the home of thousands of artists, singers, and celebrities **from a great variety of backgrounds**. More than 50 million tourists travel there each year to enjoy the amazing sights and sounds. With so much to offer, it's easy to see why the city's nickname is the Big Apple.

New York City has long had an important place in American history. For millions of immigrants in the 19th and 20th centuries, it was their point of entry into the USA. Greeting them was the Statue of Liberty, a gift from France to the USA in 1886. The city is also the home of the United Nations, the New York Stock Exchange, and the offices of many international companies.

The city **is made up of** five sections, or "boroughs": Manhattan, Brooklyn, Queens, the Bronx, and Staten Island. Although the city is spread out, its 8.4 million residents **can easily get around** on the subway system, which has 26 routes and 468 stations. Every year, more than 1.6 billion riders use the system.

There is plenty to see and do in the city that never sleeps. People love visiting the Empire State Building, Central Park, and Rockefeller Center. Plus, there are great museums like the Met and MoMA. Attending shows on Broadway, enjoying concerts at Lincoln Center, taking in games at famous stadiums, and eating at fancy restaurants are also popular with locals and tourists.

Many of these activities are expensive, **as are** hotels. Spending $300 a night in Manhattan is common. But **one of the best things about New York City is free** – walking around interesting neighborhoods like Greenwich Village and Chinatown. **Each neighborhood has its**

own character, but they all **have one thing in common**. Though their residents may come from many countries and cultures, they're all proud to call themselves New Yorkers.

翻譯

紐約市有一種獨特的魅力。這裡是成千上萬來自各種不同背景的藝術家、歌手和名人的家。每年有超過 5000 萬名觀光客來到這座城市，欣賞它的壯麗景色與多彩文化，因此，不難理解為什麼它會被稱為「大蘋果」。

紐約市在美國歷史上一直佔有重要地位。19 世紀和 20 世紀時，數百萬移民從這裡踏入美國，迎接他們的是自由女神像——這座雕像是法國在 1886 年送給美國的禮物。此外，聯合國總部、紐約證券交易所，以及許多跨國企業的辦公室也都設立在這座城市。

紐約由五個區 (borough) 組成：曼哈頓、布魯克林、皇后區、布朗克斯和史坦頓島。雖然範圍很廣，但 840 萬名居民依靠地鐵系統穿梭其中。紐約地鐵擁有 26 條路線、468 個車站，每年載運超過 16 億人次。

這座「不夜城」有無數好玩好看的地方。人們喜歡參觀帝國大廈、中央公園和洛克菲勒中心，也可以到大都會博物館和現代藝術博物館欣賞世界級展覽。觀賞百老匯的演出、在林肯中心欣賞音樂會、在著名體育場觀看比賽以及在高檔餐廳用餐也相當受到當地人和遊客的喜愛。

當然，紐約的娛樂與住宿不便宜，特別是曼哈頓，住宿一晚 300 美元相當常見。不過，這座城市最棒的一件事是免費的——那就是漫步在富有特色的街區，如格林威治村和唐人街。每個街區都有自己的風格，但有一點是相同的——無論來自哪個國家、哪種文化，住在這裡的人都以「我是紐約客」為榮。

PLUS! 主題實用詞彙精選

☐ the home of something 表示：某地以某事物聞名，或是某事物的起源地。
☐ have something to offer 有其獨特的吸引力、有值得提供的東西、有其價值
☐ New York is the city that never sleeps. 紐約夜未眠。

New York

練習 A：用英文表達 Phrase in Action

用以下關鍵短語作為句子重點提示，試著用英文表達每一句話。不一定只有一種說法！

1 come from diverse/various/different backgrounds
超過 800 萬人生活在紐約市，他們來自各種不同的背景。

2 is made up of
約翰・甘迺迪表演藝術中心是個充滿活力的文化中心，匯聚了藝術家、行政人員和專業技術人員。

3 can easily get around
在紐約，你只需要一張地鐵卡和一雙舒服的鞋子，就能隨心所欲地到處走。

4 Each neighborhood has its own character
紐約每個區都有自己的風格特色。SoHo 有很多藝廊跟設計感十足的店；Harlem 是聽現場爵士、品嚐美國南方黑人傳統美食的好地方；要是想吃港式點心的話，去 Chinatown 一定不會讓你失望的。

> 1～4 這些短語是在描寫城市或社區特色。

5 as are
紐約的博物館是世界知名的，那些不起眼的小餐館也一樣遠近馳名。

6 one of the best things about
紐約最棒的一點就是它的多元。這裡什麼都有，不管你是誰，都能找到適合自己的東西。

> 5～7 這些短語用於指出不同事物之間的共通點或類似之處。

7 have one thing in common
是什麼讓紐約成為紐約？是人。來自四面八方的人聚在這裡，雖然背景各異，但都有一種共通的特質，為了在這座城市立足，必須具備的那股韌性。

162

New York

MP3 54

練習 B：記憶挑戰 Phrase Recall!

以下是練習 A 各句子的參考英文說法，但關鍵短語不見了！你還記得它的中文怎麼說嗎？

Reference Only – Not the Only Way!

1 (來自不同的背景)
Over 8 million people live in New York City. They come from a great variety of backgrounds.

2 (   )
The Kennedy Center, a thriving cultural hub, is made up of artists, administrators, and trade professionals.

3 (   )
In New York, you can easily get around with just a MetroCard and a good pair of walking shoes.

4 (   )
Each neighborhood in New York has its own character. SoHo is all about galleries and boutique shopping. Harlem is the place for live jazz and amazing soul food. And if you feel like some dim sum, Chinatown is the place to go.

5 (   )
The museums in New York are world-famous, as are its holes-in-the-wall.

6 (   )
One of the best things about New York is its diversity. There's something for everyone.

7 (   )
What makes New York New York? It's the people. They come from all walks of life but share one thing in common: a certain grit necessary to make it in this city.

TOPIC 14 紐約

Let's Chat!

練習 C：靈活應用 Phrase Remix!
同樣的短語，放進生活其他情境中應用看看！
你也可以試著造自己的句子！

1 from a great variety of backgrounds
我們這個團體聚了來自不同背景的人，所以每次聚會都能聊到很多新鮮、有趣的東西。

2 is made up of
這件作品尺寸為 60 x 96 英寸，以藝術家的母親命名，由玻璃磚組合而成。

3 get around
每到週末，我喜歡騎腳踏車四處走走，這是以自己的步調欣賞城市的最佳方式。

4 Each ___ has its own character
每個節日都有自己的特色，展現出慶祝它的人的文化背景。

5 as are
兒童美術課充滿了創意活力，烹飪課也是如此，它透過食物的樂趣將人們聚集在一起。

6 one of the best things about
養狗最棒的事情之一就是每天回家都能看到牠搖著尾巴迎接你。

7 have one thing in common
所有成功人士都有一個共同點，他們從不停止學習。

Let's Chat!

MP3 55

練習 D：記憶挑戰 Phrase Recall!

以下是練習 C 各句子的參考英文說法，但關鍵短語不見了，而且還變長了！試著用你的話來描述這些被標示的語言段！

*Reference Only – Not the Only Way!

1 (　　　　　　　　　　)
Our community brings together people from a great variety of backgrounds, so every meeting is full of fresh perspectives and stories.

2 (　　　　　　　　)
The 60 by 96-inch piece, titled after the artist's mother, is made up of glass tiles.

3 (　　　　　　　)
On weekends, I love getting around by bike. It's the best way to see the city at your own pace.

4 (　　　　　　　　　　)
Each festival has its own character, reflecting the cultural background of those who celebrate it.

5 (　　　　　　　)
The kids' art class is full of creative energy, as are the cooking workshops that bring people together through the joy of food.

6 (　　　　　　　　　　　)
One of the best things about having a dog is coming home to a wagging tail everyday.

7 (　　　　　　　　　　　　)
All successful people have one thing in common. They never stop learning.

Expand! (關鍵短語 1 + 1 > 2 !!)

MP3 56

看看本單元學過的關鍵短語，還可以延伸出哪些相關說法呢？繼續擴充你的口說及寫作素材吧！

① from a great variety of backgrounds 來自各種不同的背景
people from all walks of life 來自各行各業的人們
from two different cultures 來自兩種不同文化

Volunteers from a great variety of backgrounds came together to help rebuild the community after the earthquake.
來自各種不同背景的志工齊聚一堂，幫助地震後的社區重建。

During a local Earth Day event, the volunteers **engage with strangers from all walks of life**.
在當地的地球日活動中，志工與來自各行各業的陌生人交流。

The restaurant is run by **a couple from two different cultures**, blending Asian and Mediterranean flavors in their dishes.
這間餐廳由來自不同文化的伴侶經營，將亞洲與地中海風味融合在菜餚中。

② get around 四處走走、旅行遊歷、活動
from place to place / from house to house 到處、從這一地到另一地

During the weekdays, **I commute to work**, but on weekends, I like to **get around the city** and explore new places.
平日我通勤上下班，但週末我喜歡四處走走，探索新的地方。

The boy went **from place to place** asking if anyone had seen his cat.
那個男孩到處詢問有沒有人看見他的貓咪。

3
  be the home of 發源地
  be home to ……的所在 / 歸屬

Italy **is the home of** the Renaissance.
義大利是文藝復興的發源地。

Paris **is home to** many luxury brands.
巴黎有眾多精品名牌。

4
  as are 也是如此
  widely accepted/essential/enjoyable, as are...
  the same goes for someone/something 也一樣、同樣適用

Good friends are necessary, **as are morning coffee and a bit of laughter every day**.
好朋友是不可或缺的,早上一杯咖啡和每天一點笑聲也是一樣。

You should take this seriously, and **the same goes for** the rest of you.
你應該要認真看待這件事情,其他人也一樣。

5
  one of the best things about 最棒的一件事就是……
  what makes... special is 讓……特別之處是

One of the best things about living in a big city is the food. You are spoiled for choice and there's always something new to try. **What makes it special is** how fusion cuisine brings cultures together and creates new traditions.
住在大城市最棒的事之一就是美食。選擇多到讓人難以抉擇,而且總是能找到新開的店。特別的地方是,無國界料理不僅將不同文化融合在一起,還創造了新的傳統。

6 **have one thing in common** 有一個共通點
a universal truth 放諸四海皆準的道理

Strong teams **have one thing in common**. They hold a shared belief that no one succeeds alone, which **is a universal truth** in both work and life.
強大的團隊都有一個共通點，他們都相信光靠一個人的力量無法成功，而這無論在工作還是生活中都是普遍的道理。

TOPIC 15

London: A City of Timeless Charm

倫敦：風華萬千的城市

倫敦。

泰晤士河

雙層巴士

大笨鐘

Reading

MP3 57

閱讀以下文章，粗體字部分是本文的關鍵短語，先想想它們的意思及用法，再跟著引導進行更多字彙擴充練習！

London, one of the world's great cities, has many strengths. One is its ability to grow and **change with the times**. Over the centuries, the city has faced many challenges, **yet it has met them all head on**. Along the way, England's capital has developed into one of the world's most diverse cities. It is home to people from many cultures, adding to the city's rich heritage. The Romans first developed the area 2,000 years ago, founding a town which they called Londinium. In the 11th century, the city, whose name had been shortened to London, became England's capital. Over the centuries, new leaders **added their own touches**. Some built great churches. Others built grand palaces. Sites like the Tower of London, Westminster Abbey, and Buckingham Palace became part of the city's identity.

However, London's history is not only one of progress. The city has gone through terrible crises. In the 14th century, one-third of the population died from a horrible disease – the Black Death. In 1666, 80% of the city burned down during the Great Fire of London. Then, during the early years of World War II, much of the city was destroyed by German bombers. Yet **time after time**, the city has **stood tall** and rebuilt itself.

London is now a leading cultural center. There are many top museums such as the National Gallery and the British Museum. The performing arts are also alive and well, with concerts and plays to suit every culture lover's taste. For more casual entertainment, people can dance **to their heart's content** at night clubs. Sports lovers also have a lot to choose from, such as Wimbledon, a major tennis event held every year. Plus, don't forget the dining scene. Six thousand restaurants serve food from more than 70 countries.

A great way to get a feeling for this amazing city is by taking a ride on the London Eye. Thirty-minute trips carry people 500 feet into the air, offering excellent views. You can also see the sights on a "double decker" bus. Or, to travel quickly from A to B, you can ride the Tube, London's subway system. Its 535 trains carry around 3.5 million riders a day. London's 8.3 million residents come together to **form the heart and soul of** the city. They include people from many cultures and world regions, such as Asia, Africa, and the Caribbean. In festivals like the Notting Hill Carnival, they celebrate their diverse backgrounds. **Generation after generation**, every Londoner adds to the spirit of the ever-changing city.

翻譯

倫敦，作為世界偉大的城市之一，擁有許多優勢。其中之一就是它能夠隨著時代的變遷而成長與改變。在幾個世紀的歷史中，這座城市面臨了許多挑戰，但它總是迎難而上。隨著時間推移，英國的首都已發展成為世界上最具多樣性的城市之一。來自各種文化背景的人們在此落腳，為這座城市增添了豐富的色彩。大約兩千年前，羅馬人首次開發了這個地方，並建立了一個名為倫敦尼亞 (Londinium) 的城鎮。到了 11 世紀，這座城市的名字縮短為倫敦，並成為英格蘭的首都。在接下來的幾個世紀中，不同的領袖們都曾經改造過這座城市，有些人建造了偉大的教堂，有些人則建造了宏偉的宮殿，像倫敦塔、西敏寺與白金漢宮這些地標，逐漸成為這座城市身分的一部分。

然而，倫敦的歷史不僅僅是進步的象徵。這座城市也經歷過許多可怕的危機。在 14 世紀，三分之一的人口死於可怕的瘟疫——黑死病。1666 年，倫敦大火燒毀了整座城市的 80%。之後，在第二次世界大戰初期，倫敦又有大片區域被德國轟炸機摧毀。然而，無論經歷多少次挑戰，倫敦總能重建自己，堅強屹立。

如今，倫敦已經成為世界的文化中心，這裡有許多頂級博物館，如國家美術館和大英博物館，表演藝術也蓬勃發展，這裡有各式各樣的音樂會和戲劇，滿足每一位文化愛好者的品味。如果想要更輕鬆一點的娛樂，夜店能讓人盡情唱跳狂歡。喜歡體育的人們也有很多選擇，比如每年舉辦的溫布頓網球賽。此外，倫敦的美食也非常精彩，總共有六千多家餐廳，提供來自七十多個國家的美食。

想要更好地體驗這座令人驚豔的城市，搭乘倫敦眼是一個不錯的方式。這段為期三十分鐘的旅程將人帶到 500 英尺的高空，提供絕佳的觀景視角。你也可以在雙層巴士上欣賞倫敦的美。或者，如果需要快速從甲地到乙地，則可以乘坐倫敦地鐵，總計 535 列列車每天運送約 350 萬名乘客。830 萬倫敦居民才是這座城市的靈魂所在。他們來自世界各地，不同文化背景，如亞洲、非洲和加勒比海地區。在像諾丁丘嘉年華這樣的節慶中，人們以盛大的慶祝活動彰顯文化多樣性。走過無數世世代代，每一個倫敦人都為這座不斷變化的城市注入滿滿的活力。

Lodon

練習 A：用英文表達 *Phrase in Action*

用以下關鍵短語作為句子重點提示，試著用英文表達每一句話。不一定只有一種說法！

1 head-on
倫敦的歷史可不是一帆風順，從二戰期間的倫敦大轟炸到景氣衰退，這座城市始終迎難而上。

> 1～2 用於描述城市、人物或是企業組織等等，面對挑戰不退縮、積極回應危機的態度。

2 stand tall
聖保羅大教堂經過幾個世紀的火災、轟炸和戰爭，如今依然巍然聳立。它是倫敦堅韌不拔的象徵。

> 3～5 用於鋪陳歷史脈絡、文化演進、代代延續的場景。

3 change with the times
1951 年前，南岸主要是工業區，現已從一片沼澤地轉變為文化中心，見證了時代的發展與變遷。

4 time after time
倫敦一次又一次地證明自己是一座永遠不失魅力的城市。

5 generation after generation
從過去到現在，下午茶一直是英國生活的一部分。

6 add their own touches
波羅市場是倫敦最古老的食品市場之一。這麼多年來，商販們為這裡增添了自己獨特的色彩。

7 to your heart's content
週末市集可以讓你盡情購物，哪怕只是悠閒地到處走走看看，都非常值得一遊。

8 form the heart and soul of
酒吧和劇院是倫敦西區的核心與靈魂。這裡是你放鬆和與朋友聚會的地方。

Lodon

MP3 58

練習 B：記憶挑戰 Phrase Recall!

以下是練習 A 各句子的參考英文說法，但關鍵短語不見了！你還記得它的中文怎麼說嗎？

Reference Only – Not the Only Way!

1 (　　　　　　　　　　)
London's history isn't all sunshine and rainbows. From the Blitz during WWII to economic downturns, the city has met every challenge head-on.

2 (　　　　　　　)
St. Paul's Cathedral has survived fires, bombings, and wars over the centuries. Now, it still stands tall. The iconic landmark has been a symbol of London's resilience.

3 (　　　　　　　　　　)
Before 1951, South Bank was largely industrial, and it has transformed from a marshy landscape into a cultural hub. It surely is an example of a place that has changed with the times.

4 (　　　　　　　)
Time after time, London has proven itself as a city that never loses its charm.

5 (　　　　　　　　　)
Generation after generation, afternoon tea has been a part of British life.

6 (　　　　　　　　　)
Borough Market is one of London's oldest food markets. Over time, traders have added their own touches to the place.

7 (　　　　　　　　　)
At the Sunday market, you can shop to your heart's content. Or, you can simply take a window-shopping tour. It's worth a visit.

8 (　　　　　　　　　　)
Pubs and theaters form the heart and soul of London's West End. It's where you go to relax and catch up with friends.

TOPIC **15** 倫敦　　173

Let's Chat!

練習 C：靈活應用 Phrase Remix!
同樣的短語，放進生活其他情境中應用看看！
你也可以試著造自己的句子！

1 head-on
忽視問題不會讓它們消失，你必須正面迎接挑戰。

2 stand tall
幾百年來，那棵老樹依然屹立在花園中央，像是守護者一樣。

3 change with the times
這家餐廳與時俱進，從原本只供應簡單的家常菜，如今以創意料理聞名。

4 added their own touches
設計師在飯店大廳加入了自己的巧思，為賓客打造難忘的體驗。

5 generation after generation
這家烘焙坊在鎮上開很久了，一直以來，每到聖誕節，大家都會買它的餅乾送家人朋友。

6 time after time
人們總是嘲笑他，但一次又一次，事實證明他是對的。

7 to your heart's content
孩子們在公園裡玩得不亦樂乎，空氣中充滿了他們無憂無慮的笑聲，彷彿整個世界都是他們的天地。

8 form the heart and soul of
那家小書店是這條街的靈魂所在。人們喜歡在這裡停留片刻，細細品味寧靜的氛圍。

Let's Chat!

MP3 59

練習 D：記憶挑戰 Phrase Recall!

以下是練習C各句子的參考英文說法，但關鍵短語不見了，而且還變長了！試著用你的話來描述這些被標示的語言段！

*Reference Only - Not the Only Way!

1 (　　　　　　　　　　　)
Ignoring the problems doesn't make them go away. You have to face the challenges head-on.

2 (　　　　　　　　　　　)
After centuries, the old tree stands tall in the center of the garden, like a guardian.

3 (　　　　　　　　　　　　　)
This restaurant has changed with the times. It only offered a simple family-style menu, but now it's known for its fusion dishes.

4 (　　　　　　　　　　　　　)
The designers added their own touches to the hotel lobby to create a memorable experience for their guests.

5 (　　　　　　　　　　　　　)
The bakery has been in town forever. Generation after generation, people have bought its cookies as gifts for family and friends at Christmas.

6 (　　　　　　　　　)
People would laugh at what he said, but time after time, he was proven right.

7 (　　　　　　　　　　　)
The children played to their heart's content in the park. Their carefree laughter filled the air, as if the whole world belonged to them.

8 (　　　　　　　　　　　　　)
That little bookstore forms the heart and soul of the street. People love stopping by and enjoying the quiet vibe.

TOPIC 15 倫敦　175

Expand!（關鍵短語 1 + 1 > 2 !!） MP3 60

看看本單元學過的關鍵短語，還可以延伸出哪些相關說法呢？繼續擴充你的口說及寫作素材吧！

❶
meet (something) head-on 直面某事
take the bull by the horns 大膽應對困難
overcome difficulties/obstacles/problems 克服所有困境

When facing setbacks, they didn't back down. **They met them all head on.**
即使情況變得艱難，他們沒有退縮，而是迎難而上。

If I were her, I wouldn't be able to **take the bull by the horns**.
如果我是她，我恐怕無法那麼勇敢地直面困難。

Even when things got tough, **they managed to overcome all the difficulties**.
即使在困難時刻，他們仍然設法克服所有的挑戰。

❷
stand tall 昂首佇立
hold/stand your ground 堅守立場
remain unshaken 保持不動搖

Even when life gets rough, **stand tall**.
即使人生很難，也要挺直腰桿，堅定前行。

Even when the storm raged, **the old lighthouse remained unshaken**.
即使風暴肆虐，那座老燈塔依然屹立不搖。

During the meeting, even though her colleagues disagreed with her idea, **she managed to hold her ground**.
在會議中，儘管同事們不同意她的想法，她仍然必須堅守她的立場。

change with the times 與時俱進
❸ **keep up with the times** 跟上時代
keep pace with 跟上

Fashion trends change with the times, but classic styles will never grow old.
時尚潮流與時俱進,但經典款式卻歷久彌新。

To stay competitive in today's fast-paced world, **businesses need to keep up with the times**.
為了在今天這個快速變化的世界中保持競爭力,企業必須要能跟上時代的腳步。

The law **has not kept pace with** the rapid development of technology.
現行法律未能跟上科技發展快速的腳步。

added their own touches 加入自己的特色
❹ **put/leave one's stamp on** 留下印記、發揮影響力
injected personality into 讓某事更具個人特色

When the young couple opened the boutique, **they really added their own touches**. From the layout to the music in the background, **they injected their personality into every detail**.
這對年輕夫妻開設這間精品店時,他們真的融入了自己的風格。從空間設計到播放的音樂,每一個細節都展現他們自己的特色。

Over the years, **she has left her stamp on the fashion world** with her unique designs.
多年來,她憑藉獨特的設計在時尚界留下了自己的印記。

to your heart's content 盡情地
❺ **to the fullest** 盡情地

They danced **to their heart's content** and enjoyed the music **to the fullest**.
他們盡情地跳舞,徹底享受音樂帶來的樂趣。

> **time after time** 一再地
> ❻ **over and over again** 反覆地
> **again and again** 一次又一次

The puppy chased the ball over and over again, not getting tired of the game.
小狗反覆地追著球跑，絲毫不覺得疲倦。

Again and again, people return to the old bookstore. It offers an escape from the hustle and bustle.
一次又一次，人們回到那家老書店。它提供了一個遠離喧囂的避風港。

> **form the heart and soul of** 構成……的核心與靈魂
> ❼ **be the backbone of** 是……的支柱
> **be the cornerstone of** 是……的基石

Honesty and integrity **form the heart of** the organization.
誠實與正直是這個機構的核心價值。

Teachers **are the backbone of** our education system.
教師是教育體系中重要的支柱。

Trust **is the cornerstone of** every healthy relationship.
信任是良好關係的基石。

> **generation after generation** 世世代代
> ❽ **for generations** 代代相傳
> **pass something down** 代代相傳／傳承

Traditions like these **have been celebrated for generations**.
像這樣的傳統已經傳承了好幾代。

This necklace has been **passed down** from generation to generation.
這條項鍊在家族裡代代相傳。

Science, Innovation & Future Trends

科普與未來趨勢

PART 5

TOPIC 16

Yoga: Ancient Wisdom, Modern Healing
瑜伽：古老智慧，現代療癒

瑜伽。
內在平靜
紓壓
冥想
調息法

Reading

MP3 61

閱讀以下文章，粗體字部分是本文的關鍵短語，先想想它們的意思及用法，再跟著引導進行更多字彙擴充練習！

Many of us lead fast and busy lives. Computers, cell phones, and other tools make our lives easier, but we're still under a lot of stress. To help cope with the pressure, **people are turning to an ancient practice**, yoga. It can improve one's health and lead to a sense of inner peace.

Yoga means "union." Its goal is to **bring** the body, mind, and spirit **into harmony**. The practice began in India a very long time ago. It was first written about more than 2,000 years ago in an important book, the *Bhagavad Gita*. Over time, many branches of yoga were developed. In modern India, the most popular branch is Bhakti Yoga. **Like** other types of yoga, it is closely connected to the Hindu religion.

Outside of India, many people, **no matter what their religion is**, have taken up yoga. The Hatha style attracts people who want to exercise. People sit and stand in different poses, called "asanas." Some are very simple. Others take years of study to master. In Hatha Yoga, attention is also placed on breathing practices, called "pranayama," and on meditation.

Yoga **has a long list of benefits**. It improves physical strength, raises energy levels, and makes a person more flexible. On top of that, yoga can help with problems like back pain, and it can even help someone lose weight. What's more, yoga can lower one's stress level and lead to a greater sense of calm.

With all these benefits, it's no wonder there are yoga classes in so many countries. Some new styles have even been developed outside of India. As we push into the 21st century, we will surely discover many incredible new things. It's interesting that we can still learn so much from an ancient practice like yoga.

翻譯

許多人過著忙碌而且步調很快的生活。電腦、手機等科技雖然讓生活更加方便，卻也讓我們承受很大的壓力。為了紓解壓力，人們開始轉向一種古老的練習——瑜伽。它不僅有助於改善健康，還能帶來內在的平靜。

瑜伽的意思是「合一」，其目標是讓身體、心靈與精神達到和諧。瑜伽在很久以前起源於印度，最早可追溯至 2000 多年前的《薄伽梵歌》。後來，瑜伽發展出許多不同的分支。在現代印度，最流行的是「奉愛瑜伽」(Bhakti Yoga)，與其他瑜伽流派一樣，它與印度教有很深的關聯。

在印度以外，無論宗教信仰如何，越來越多人開始練習瑜伽。其中，「哈達瑜伽」(Hatha Yoga) 特別受到喜愛運動者的青睞。這種瑜伽包含各種坐姿與站姿，被稱為「體位法」(asanas)，有些動作簡單易學，而有些則需要多年練習才能掌握。哈達瑜伽也強調呼吸練習「調息法」(pranayama) 與冥想，來幫助身心放鬆。

瑜伽帶來眾多好處，除了增強體能、提升精力，還能讓身體柔軟度更好。此外，它有助於舒緩背痛，甚至對減重也有所幫助。更重要的是，瑜伽能有效降低壓力，使人獲得內心的平靜。

憑藉這些好處，瑜伽課程如今遍布世界各地，甚至在印度以外還發展出許多新的流派。隨著我們邁向 21 世紀，將會發現更多令人驚奇的新事物，但有趣的是，我們依然能從這項古老的練習中，汲取寶貴的智慧。

PLUS! 主題實用詞彙精選

☐ lead a busy, normal, quiet, etc. life 過著……的生活
☐ inner peace 內心平靜

Yoga

練習 A：用英文表達 Phrase in Action

用以下關鍵短語作為句子重點提示，試著用英文表達每一句話。不一定只有一種說法！

1 turn to someone/something
超過六成的研究參與者表示，雖然他們一開始是為了健康而尋求瑜伽的幫助，但隨著時間過去，讓他們持續練習的主因已經改變。對多數人來說，現在更在意的是那種內心的平靜與安定感。

2 Like…,
像其他有助於減壓的活動一樣，瑜伽也能幫助提升心理健康。如果你持之以恆地練習，從頭到腳都能感覺越來越好。

> 1～2 的短語用來開啟主題、說明背景、引導讀者進入某個觀點。

3 no matter what/when/why
不管你有多久沒練習了，隨時都能回來繼續。

4 bring… into harmony
瑜伽的呼吸練習能讓情緒與思緒穩定下來。

> 3～6 的短語用來描述細節，提供佐證，解釋其影響層面。

5 has a long list of benefits
這項古老的練習好處多多，它能幫助緩解背痛，增強力量與柔軟度，還能舒壓。上瑜伽課還能讓你在團體中一起放鬆、互相支持。

6 with all these benefits
正因為這些好處，難怪越來越多公司開始為員工提供瑜伽課程。

Yoga

MP3 62

練習 B：記憶挑戰 **Phrase Recall!**

以下是練習 A 各句子的參考英文說法，但關鍵短語不見了！你還記得它的中文怎麼說嗎？

*Reference Only – Not the Only Way!

1（雖然他們一開始是為了健康而尋求瑜伽的幫助）
More than 60 percent of the study's participants said that while they initially turned to yoga for the health benefits, their main reason for sticking with it has shifted over time. For most, it's now more about feeling calm and inner peace.

2（   ）
Like other activities that help reduce stress, yoga can help improve our mental well-being. If you're practicing regularly, you can feel better from head to toe.

3（   ）
No matter how long you're away from your practice, you can always come back and pick up right where you left off.

4（   ）
Breathing exercises in yoga can bring feelings and thoughts into harmony.

5（   ）
This ancient practice has a long list of benefits. It helps relieve back pain, improves strength and flexibility, and helps you manage stress. Participating in yoga classes even provides an environment for group healing and support.

6（   ）
With all these benefits, no wonder more workplaces are introducing yoga sessions for employees.

TOPIC 16 瑜伽：古老智慧，現代療癒

Let's Chat!

練習 C：靈活應用 Phrase Remix!

同樣的短語，放進生活其他情境中應用看看！
你也可以試著造自己的句子！

1 turn to someone/something
想像一下，當遇到困難時沒有任何一個人可以求助。對許多老年人來說，這就是他們的日常生活。該慈善機構正在努力確保沒有人會面臨這種孤獨。

2 Like...,
像大多數父母一樣，我得想辦法兼顧工作和家庭。我希望今天分享的內容能給大家一些幫助。不過，說到底，沒有什麼放諸四海皆準的解決方法。

3 no matter what/when/why
不管發生什麼事，我奶奶每天早上都堅持要去散步。

4 bring... into harmony
工作時聽音樂能讓創造力與專注力保持平衡，讓事情變得沒那麼有壓力。

5 has a long list of benefits
睡前閱讀好處多多，包括減輕壓力和提升睡眠品質。

6 with all these benefits
有這麼多優點，這個產品為何如此受歡迎也就不難理解了。

Let's Chat!

MP3 63

練習 D：記憶挑戰 Phrase Recall!

以下是練習 C 各句子的參考英文說法，但關鍵短語不見了，而且還變長了！試著用你的話來描述這些被標示的語言段！
*Reference Only – Not the Only Way!

1 (　　　　　　　　　　)
Imagine **having no one to turn to** when times get tough. For many older people, that's their everyday reality. The charity is working hard to make sure no one has to face that kind of loneliness.

2 (　　　　　　　　　　)
Like most parents, I have to juggle work and family. I hope what I share today can give you some useful ideas. There's no one-size-fits-all solution, though.

3 (　　　　　　　　　　)
No matter what happens, my grandma insists on taking her morning walk every single day.

4 (　　　　　　　　　　)
Listening to music while working **can bring creativity and concentration into harmony**, making tasks feel less stressful.

5 (　　　　　　　　　　)
Reading before bed has a long list of benefits, including reducing stress and improving sleep quality.

6 (　　　　　　　　　　)
With all these benefits, it's clear why this product is so popular.

TOPIC 16 瑜伽：古老智慧，現代療癒　187

Expand! (關鍵短語 1 + 1 > 2 !!)　　　MP3 64

看看本單元學過的關鍵短語，還可以延伸出哪些相關說法呢？繼續擴充你的口說及寫作素材吧！

1
turn to someone/something 尋求……的幫助支持或建議、開始去……
more and more people are choosing... 越來越多人選擇……

Why do people **turn to meditation** nowadays? Actually, it's more powerful than you think. In today's fast-paced world, it gives us a chance to pause, breathe and reset.
為什麼現在那麼多人開始練習冥想呢？其實，它的力量超乎你的想像。在如今這個步調很快的世界，冥想讓我們有機會停下來，深呼吸，重新調整自己。

More and more people are choosing to live alone.
越來越多人選擇獨居生活。

2
Like..., 如同……一樣
the same as 和……一樣

Like most teenagers, my sister spends hours on her phone.
跟大多數青少年一樣，我妹妹花很多時間在滑手機。

What a coincidence! Your idea is **the same as mine**.
好巧啊！你的想法跟我的一樣。

3
no matter what/when/why 不論何事 / 何時 / 任何原因
no matter what 無論如何
no matter how you slice it (any way you slice it)
不管從哪方面考慮、無論你怎麼看，結果都是一樣的

No matter what they say, you should believe in yourself.
無論他們怎麼說，你都應該相信自己。

I won't give up, **no matter what**.
無論如何我都不會放棄。

It's not a fair deal, **no matter how you slice it**.
無論怎麼看,這都不是一個公平的交易。

> **4** bring... into harmony 讓……達到和諧
> bridge the gap 彌平差距
> be/move/work in sync 同步

Good interior design **brings aesthetics and function into harmony**, making a space both stylish and useful. It creates a balance between comfort and efficiency, ensuring that a home feels inviting while staying organized.
好的室內設計能兼具美感與實用性,讓空間既有型又實用。在舒適與效率之間取得平衡,讓家裡溫馨而不顯擁擠。

Tablets **bridge the gap** between smartphones and laptops so we get the best of both worlds.
平板電腦彌補了智慧型手機和筆記型電腦之間的差距,讓我們可以同時享受兩種產品各自的好處。

The two dancers practiced for a long time so they could **move in sync**.
兩名舞者花了很長時間練習,才能做到動作完全同步。

> **5** a long list of 為數眾多的……
> a great deal of 大量的……

My partner worked as a real estate agent for ten years and made **a great deal of money**.
我的另一半做房地產十年,賺了很多錢。

The experimental cancer drug has **a long list of** side effects.
這個試驗中的癌症新藥有非常多副作用。

TOPIC **16** 瑜伽:古老智慧,現代療癒　189

with all these benefits 有這些好處

❻ **That's why... is becoming more popular.** 這就是為什麼……越來越受歡迎。

with the benefit of hindsight/experience 事後回顧、經驗之後才明白

It helps rehydrate the skin, fights fine lines and wrinkles, and keeps your skin looking radiant. The best part is you don't need to break the bank. **With all these benefits**, it's no wonder the anti-aging cream is the bestseller this year.
它幫助皮膚保濕，對抗老化細紋，讓你的肌膚維持亮麗光采。最棒的是，你不需要花大錢。有這些優點，難怪這款抗老霜成為今年的暢銷產品。

People are looking for healthier alternatives to soda. **That's why** sparkling water **is becoming more popular**.
許多人開始尋找比汽水更健康的選擇，這也是氣泡水越來越受歡迎的原因。

With the benefit of hindsight, the manager saw where he had gone wrong.
事後想來，經理才明白自己哪裡做錯了。

TOPIC 17

Forensic Science
鑑識科學

CSI
犯罪現場。
破案
指紋
彈道學

DNA吻合

Reading

MP3 65

閱讀以下文章，粗體字部分是本文的關鍵短語，先想想它們的意思及用法，再跟著引導進行更多字彙擴充練習！

Criminals are finding it harder to hide from the law. That's because **they're up against** a special type of scientist. Trained with the latest technology, "forensic scientists" work with police departments. Using microscopes and computers, they help solve even the most difficult cases.

Scientific techniques have been used in police work for centuries. In 1248, a book from China listed ways to figure out what weapon was used in a crime. Several centuries later, in 1775, a Swedish scientist learned **how to tell** if poison was used to murder someone. Then, in 1835, police officers in England started using ballistics, a technique to match a bullet with the gun it was fired from.

Today's forensic scientists are **nothing short of** crime solving masters. On **the front lines** are crime scene investigators. They collect fingerprints, blood, hair, dirt, and other items at crime scenes. This type of work has been made famous by TV shows like *CSI*. Although the working methods used on these shows don't exactly match those of real scientists, some are similar.

The items gathered from a crime scene are studied at a lab. Using a comparison microscope, scientists can check if a hair sample matches a suspect's hair. Also, DNA taken from a drop of blood can be fed into a computer. The sample is compared to the information in a database. **If there's a match**, it's evidence that a suspect was at the scene. **It may be enough to prove** that he or she committed a crime.

To carry out these difficult jobs, forensic scientists need to be highly skilled. They often have degrees in biology or chemistry. Many also have knowledge of police work. Their work isn't always as exciting as that shown on TV dramas, but it is still very important. These crime fighters in white lab coats help police officers catch more criminals. That makes our cities and streets safer.

翻譯

隨著鑑識科學的進步，犯罪越來越難逃過法律制裁，因為罪犯面對的是一群專業人士──鑑識科學家。這些專家接受了最先進的技術訓練，與警方密切合作，運用顯微鏡、電腦等工具，協助破解最棘手的案件。

科學技術早在幾個世紀前便被運用於警察辦案。1248 年，中國的一本書記載了如何辨識犯罪時使用的武器；幾百年後的 1775 年，瑞典一名科學家發現如何檢測毒藥是否被用來行凶；而在 1835 年，英國警方開始使用彈道學，透過比對子彈與槍支來尋找證據。

如今，鑑識科學家堪稱破案專家，特別是在第一線的犯罪現場調查員，他們負責蒐集指紋、血跡、毛髮、土壤等關鍵證據。電視劇《CSI 犯罪現場》讓這項工作廣為人知，雖然劇中的破案手法與現實中的科學方法並不完全相符，但仍有一定的相似之處。

從犯罪現場蒐集的證據會被送往實驗室進一步分析。例如，科學家可以使用比較顯微鏡來檢查毛髮樣本是否與嫌疑人相符，或是透過血跡中的 DNA，與資料庫中的數據進行比對。如果找到吻合的結果，就證明嫌疑人曾出現在案發現場，這足以成為破案的關鍵證據。

要勝任這項複雜且精細的工作，鑑識科學家必須具備高度專業的技能。他們通常擁有生物學或化學的學位，並且對警方的辦案方式有一定的了解。雖然他們的工作不像影視劇情般驚心動魄，但卻至關重要。這些穿著白色實驗袍的「無名英雄」，幫助警方逮捕罪犯，使我們的城市與街道變得更安全。

PLUS! 主題實用詞彙精選

- crime scene 犯罪現場
- forensic science 鑑識科學、刑事偵查學
- commit a crime 犯罪
- solve a case 破案

Forensic Science

練習 A：用英文表達 Phrase in Action

用以下關鍵短語作為句子重點提示，試著用英文表達每一句話。不一定只有一種說法！

1 if there's a match
如果現場發現的指紋與資料庫中的指紋比對吻合，調查人員就能在幾分鐘內確認犯罪嫌疑人的身份。

2 it may be enough to
一根頭髮可能足以證明某人曾經出現在案發現場。

📎 1～2 的短語是描述條件與假設性的情境。

3 they're up against
鑑識專家知道，他們面對的是試圖掩蓋痕跡的罪犯，因此在尋找證據時，絕不放過任何一絲線索。

4 the front lines
犯罪現場調查員站在第一線，蒐集纖維、鞋印及其他可能成為關鍵線索的證據。

5 nothing short of
鑑識科學在現代刑事調查中無疑是不可或缺的。

6 how to tell
鑑識專家學會如何根據腳印判斷某人是走路還是跑步。腳印之間的距離可以顯示他們的速度，而腳印的深度則能暗示這個人的體重。

7 to carry out
為了進行準確的 DNA 分析，鑑識實驗室必須確保所有樣本沒有受到污染。

Forensic Science

MP3 66

練習 B：記憶挑戰 Phrase Recall!

以下是練習A各句子的參考英文說法，但關鍵短語不見了！你還記得它的中文怎麼說嗎？

*Reference Only – Not the Only Way!

1 (　　　　　　　)
If there's a match between fingerprints found at a crime scene and those in the database, investigators can identify a suspect within minutes.

2 (　　　　　　　　)
A single strand of hair **may be enough to** confirm that someone was present at the crime scene.

3 (　　　　　　　　　)
Forensic experts know **they're up against criminals** who try to cover their tracks so they leave no stone unturned in the search for evidence.

4 (　　　　　　　　)
Crime scene investigators are **on the front lines**, collecting fibers, shoe prints, and other evidence that could lead to a breakthrough.

5 (　　　　　　)
Forensic science **is nothing short of** indispensable in modern criminal investigations.

6 (　　　　　　)
Forensic experts **learn how to tell** if someone was walking or running based on their footprints. The distance between the prints can indicate their speed, and the depth of the prints can suggest the person's weight.

7 (　　　　　　)
To carry out a proper DNA analysis, forensic labs must ensure that all samples are handled carefully to avoid contamination.

Let's Chat!

練習 C：靈活應用 Phrase Remix!
同樣的短語，放進生活其他情境中應用看看！
你也可以試著造自己的句子！

1 if there's a match
如果你的經歷符合職缺要求，錄取機會就更高。

2 it may be enough to
一句溫暖的話或一個微笑，或許就能讓某人的一天變得更美好。

3 we're up against
我們所面臨的問題比我們想像的更為複雜，因此我們決定與當地社區、政府以及非營利組織合作。團結起來，我們可以讓不可能成為可能。

4 nothing short of
山頂的日出簡直就是如夢似幻。

5 the front lines
她一直在最前線努力制止野生動物走私。

6 how to tell
水果攤老闆很親切，他教我如何判斷水果的成熟度。

7 to carry out
要辦好一場活動，你需要良好的規劃、團隊合作，以及對細節的講究。

196

Let's Chat!

MP3 67

練習 D：記憶挑戰 **Phrase Recall!**

以下是練習 C 各句子的參考英文說法，但關鍵短語不見了，而且還變長了！試著用你的話來描述這些被標示的語言段！

*Reference Only – Not the Only Way!

1 (　　　　　　　　　　　　　　　　　　　)
If there's a match between your experience and a job description, you're more likely to get hired.

2 (　　　　　　　　　　　　)
A small gesture, like a kind word or a smile, may be enough to brighten someone's day.

3 (　　　　　　　　　　　　)
The problems we're up against are more complicated than we imagined, so we decided to partner with local communities, governments, and non-governmental organizations. Together, we can make the impossible possible.

4 (　　　　　　　　)
The view from the mountaintop at sunrise was nothing short of magical.

5 (　　　　　　　　　)
She has been working on the front lines to stop wildlife trafficking.

6 (　　　　　　　　　　)
The fruit vendor was very friendly. He showed me how to tell if the fruit was ripe.

7 (　　　　　　　　　　　　)
To carry out a successful event, you need good planning, teamwork, and attention to detail.

TOPIC 17 鑑識科學　197

Expand! (關鍵短語 1 + 1 > 2 !!)

MP3 68

看看本單元學過的關鍵短語，還可以延伸出哪些相關說法呢？繼續擴充你的口說及寫作素材吧！

① match 相配的物品、相配的兩人、旗鼓相當的對手
　a match made in heaven 天作之合
　no match for 不是對手（能力優勢等等明顯不及對方）

Everyone says that we are **a match made in heaven**. Well, I think there's no such thing as a soul mate. Marriage is hard work. Period.
每個人都說我們是<u>天作之合</u>。不過，我認為根本沒有什麼靈魂伴侶。婚姻是需要不斷努力的，簡而言之就是這樣。

We are **no match for our opponent**, but that doesn't mean we shouldn't put our best foot forward.
要比實力我們的確<u>比不過對手</u>，但這並不代表我們就不需要全力以赴。

② how to tell 要去分辨、要去看出……
　find out 發現、弄清楚
　figure out... 弄清楚……

How to tell if someone is genuinely interested in a conversation? Their body language usually doesn't lie.
<u>如何判斷</u>某人是否真心對話題感興趣？他們的肢體語言通常不會說謊。

When I was fifteen, I **found out** I was adopted.
當我十五歲時，<u>我才知道</u>自己是被領養的。

Sometimes, **it's hard to figure out** if a skincare product actually works or if it's just good marketing.
有時候，<u>很難判斷</u>一款護膚產品是否真的有效，還是只是行銷包裝得好。

3 **it may be enough to** 可能就已經足夠
do the trick 可以得到你想要的結果

It may be enough to simply listen when someone is struggling. They don't always need your advice. Sometimes, they just need someone to be there for them.
當朋友遇到困難時，你能夠好好傾聽他們的心聲就已經足夠，有時候他們需要的不是一個解決的辦法，而是想要感受到有人在身邊支持他們。

If you want to bring this dish to the next level, some lemon juice should **do the trick**.
如果你想讓這道菜更有層次，加點檸檬汁就能達到效果。

4 **they're up against** 他們正面臨……
struggle with... 與……掙扎對抗
fight against... 與……對抗

If you're **struggling with** stress, talk to someone you trust about how you're feeling. You might think, "What's the point? They won't understand." But opening up doesn't mean you're expecting them to fix you. A heart-to-heart can feel like a giant hug. It makes you feel better and gives you more energy to face the challenges yourself.
如果你正承受很大的壓力，試著跟信任的人聊聊你的感受。你可能會想，「有什麼用呢？他們根本不會懂。」但其實，開口並不代表希望他們解決問題。交心的聊天，就像是一個溫暖的擁抱，讓你感覺輕鬆一些，也會讓你更有力氣去面對那些挑戰。

This crisis we are facing is a war, but the battles are against enemies we cannot see. We are **fighting** not only **against** the contagion, but also against political selfishness and social injustice.
我們所面對的這場危機是一場戰爭，但要對抗的敵人不是肉眼可見的，我們不僅在對抗傳染病，也在對抗政治私利和社會不公。

5
> **nothing short of** 完全是……
> **it's nothing less than...** 這完全就是……
> **(There's) no two ways about it.** 這一點毫無疑問、毋庸置疑。

The food at that restaurant **was nothing short of amazing**.
那家餐廳的食物簡直令人驚艷。

What they did to you **was nothing less than** betrayal.
他們對你做的事，根本就是背叛。

I wouldn't be where I am today without my mom. **There's no two ways about it**.
如果沒有我媽媽，我今天不會是現在這樣。這一點是毫無疑問的。

6
> **the front line** 前線
> **at/in the forefront** 居於領先地位、在最前面

The research center has been **at the forefront** of several major advances in Alzheimer's research.
在阿茲海默症研究領域，這家研究中心一直走在最前端，已經有許多重大突破。

7
> **to carry out** 執行、落實
> **to make sure** 確保
> **to put... into action** 將……付諸實行

The hardest part isn't coming up with good ideas, but having the courage **to put them into action**.
最困難的部分不是想出好點子，而是有勇氣將其付諸實行。

To make sure the event runs smoothly, we need to double-check all the details in advance.
為了確保活動能順利進行，我們需要事先確認所有細節。

TOPIC 18

Franchising
加盟商機

加盟
商機無限？

權利金

Subway

品牌知名度

Reading

MP3 69

閱讀以下文章，粗體字部分是本文的關鍵短語，先想想它們的意思及用法，再跟著引導進行更多字彙擴充練習！

Well-known companies **are powered by** their names and reputations. When people walk into a Subway sandwich shop in Tokyo, Rome, or Miami, they know exactly what they're getting. Through franchising, an investor can **tap into** this brand power by opening a Subway shop of his or her own. The risk is low, and the rewards can be big. **No wonder** franchising is such a successful business model.

Franchising has been around for more than 100 years, but its popularity **took off** in the 1950s. Leading the trend were fast food restaurants like McDonald's. These days, there are franchises in more than 85 industries, including dry cleaning, hotels, and real estate. It's an important part of the global economy. In the USA alone, there are some 760,000 franchises employing 8.2 million people.

There are two sides to a franchise: the franchisor (the owner of the business system) and the franchisee (the person who licenses the system). After signing a "franchise agreement," the franchisee pays a fee. He or she also pays for equipment, supplies, and, if necessary, building costs. The total investment can range from $10,000 to $1,000,000. After the business opens, the franchisee also pays a percentage of sales revenues (called a "royalty") to the franchisor. Marketing fees must also be paid. **In return**, the franchisee receives many benefits. Training is among the most common. The franchisor offers new franchisees training in everything from dealing with customers to understanding the company's standards. The franchisor also handles advertising. On top of that, there's the all-important benefit of the brand reputation that the company has built up. All these benefits make the risk of opening a franchise much smaller than that of **starting a business from scratch**.

But a franchise can also **have drawbacks**. If a single customer at a restaurant eats something and gets sick, every franchise in the system may suffer. Running a franchise also means closely following the company's standards. As a franchisee, you have to give up a degree of independence. You have to do things the company's way and trust that the system will work.

If you want to earn a lot of money from the business, you have to work very hard. Also, don't forget: the monthly royalty must be paid, even if you are losing money. Nevertheless, there are thousands of excellent money-making opportunities in franchising. As brand recognition becomes more important in the global economy, opportunities will surely keep growing.

翻譯

知名企業的成功來自於它們的品牌形象與商譽。當人們走進位於東京、羅馬或邁阿密的 Subway（三明治連鎖店），他們知道自己會買到什麼。透過加盟，投資者可以利用這種品牌影響力，開設屬於自己的 Subway 店面。加盟的風險較低，回報卻可能相當可觀。難怪加盟成為一種非常成功的商業模式。

加盟制度已經存在超過 100 年，但直到 1950 年代才真正開始流行，而當時帶頭掀起這股風潮的，就是像麥當勞這樣的速食品牌。如今，加盟的產業已經擴展超過 85 個領域，包括乾洗店、飯店和房地產，對全球經濟影響深遠。光是在美國，就有大約 76 萬家加盟店，僱用了約 820 萬名員工。

加盟制度有兩個主要角色：總部（特許經營商，franchisor）和加盟者 (franchisee)。加盟者與總部簽訂「加盟合約」後，需要支付加盟費，還要負擔設備、原物料，甚至裝潢等費用。總投資額從 1 萬到 100 萬美元不等。店面開始營運後，加盟者還必須將部分營收（稱為「權利金」）支付給總部，此外還有行銷費用等。作為回報，加盟者可以享有很多好處，其中最重要的就是培訓。總部會提供從顧客服務到品牌標準的完整訓練。此外，廣告宣傳也由總部負責。更重要的是，加盟店可以直接受惠於品牌多年來建立的商譽。這些優勢讓加盟比起自行創業，風險低得多。

不過加盟也有一些缺點。例如，若有顧客在某家餐廳吃壞肚子，整個品牌的所有加盟店都可能受到影響。還有，開加盟店意味著必須嚴格遵守總部的規範。加盟者須放棄一部分經營自主權，完全依照總部的方式運作，並且相信這個系統能夠成功。

如果你想靠加盟賺大錢，就得投入大量心力。而且即使生意不好，依然要按時繳交權利金。儘管如此，市場上還是有許多賺錢的加盟機會。隨著品牌知名度在全球市場變得越來越重要，加盟的商機也會持續增長。

Franchising

練習 A：用英文表達

Phrase in Action

用以下關鍵短語作為句子重點提示，試著用英文表達每一句話。不一定只有一種說法！

1　are powered by
加盟商的成功來自於強大的品牌影響力和真正行得通的商業模式。

2　tap into
星巴克透過設計充滿在地特色的門市，巧妙融入並善用當地文化，同時保持全球品牌的一致性。

3　something has been around for
這家漢堡連鎖店已經開了超過 50 年，在疫情期間因為無力支撐，不得不關門。然而，現在它重振旗鼓再度開張。

> 1～5 這些短語常用來說明某個事物的運作方式、來源、歷史、或是發展趨勢。

4　take off
那家漢堡店在加設得來速服務之後，人氣暴增。

5　starting a business from scratch
從某種程度上來說，加盟比從零開始創業的風險來得低，但也不是沒有挑戰。

6　no wonder
競爭通常會導致價格下降，這正是我們當地商家所面臨的情況。再加上成本上升，難怪許多老闆都面臨現金流問題。

7　there are two sides to
每個商業決策都有兩面性。它看起來可能充滿潛力，但也會有潛在的風險。

> 6～9 這些短語著重於對事件的評價、原因結果、利弊分析。

8　in return
加盟主必須付出加盟金以及定期權利金，換來的是品牌知名度、員工訓練，以及經過市場驗證的商業模式。

9　have drawbacks
加盟連鎖店迅速崛起，因為它提供了創業的捷徑，但缺點也不少，像是嚴格的經營規範和權利金。

Franchising

MP3 70

練習 B：記憶挑戰 Phrase Recall!

以下是練習A各句子的參考英文說法，但關鍵短語不見了！你還記得它的中文怎麼說嗎？

Reference Only – Not the Only Way!

1 (成功的關鍵在於)
Franchises are powered by a strong brand and a business model that actually works.

2 (   )
Starbucks taps into local culture by designing stores that feel local but stay true to its global identity.

3 (   )
The burger chain has been around for over 50 years. During the pandemic, it had no choice but to shut up shop. Now, the once-struggling chain is making a comeback.

4 (   )
The burger joint really took off after they added a drive-through.

5 (   )
To some degree, franchising is less risky than starting a business from scratch, but it doesn't come without challenges.

6 (   )
Competition often leads to lower prices, and that's exactly what happened to our local businesses. With rising costs, (it's) no wonder many are facing cash flow issues.

7 (   )
There are two sides to every business decision. It may seem promising, but it also involves hidden risks.

8 (   )
Franchise owners need to pay an initial fee and ongoing royalties, and in return, they get brand recognition, training, and a proven business model.

9 (   )
Franchising has become popular because it offers a shortcut to business ownership, but it also has drawbacks, like strict rules and royalty fees.

TOPIC 18 加盟商機

Let's Chat!

練習 C：靈活應用 Phrase Remix!
同樣的短語，放進生活其他情境中應用看看！
你也可以試著造自己的句子！

1 are powered by
恩荷芬理工大學的學生打造了全球首輛完全以太陽能驅動的越野車。

2 tap into
如果你想變得更有創意，可以試著運用你小時候的想像力。

3 something has been around for
這座石碑已經有超過 3,000 年的歷史，但它的起源依然是個謎。

4 take off
網購在疫情期間大幅成長。

5 starting a business from scratch
白手起家創業真的很辛苦，但也是最有成就感的事之一。

6 no wonder
你每天都運動？難怪你身材這麼好！

7 there are two sides to
凡事都會有不同角度的觀點。

8 in return
你怎麼對待別人，通常也會得到相應的回報。

9 have drawbacks
在家工作很方便，但也有缺點——很難把工作跟生活區分開來。

Let's Chat!

MP3 71

練習 D：記憶挑戰 **Phrase Recall!**

以下是練習 C 各句子的參考英文說法，但關鍵短語不見了，而且還變長了！試著用你的話來描述這些被標示的語言段！
*Reference Only – Not the Only Way!

1（完全由太陽能所驅動的越野車）
A team of students at Eindhoven University of Technology has built the world's first off-road vehicle powered entirely by the sun.

2（　　　　　　　　　　）
If you want to be more creative, try tapping into your childhood imagination.

3（　　　　　　　　　　　　　　　　）
The monument has been around for over 3,000 years, but its origins are still a mystery.

4（　　　　　　　　　）
Online shopping really took off during the pandemic.

5（　　　　　　　　　）
Starting a business from scratch is tough, but it's also one of the most rewarding things you can do.

6（　　　　　　　　　）
You've been working out every day? No wonder you look so fit!

7（　　　　　　　　　）
There are two sides to every story.

8（　　　　　　　　　）
If you treat people with kindness, they will be kind to you in return.

9（　　　　　　　　　　）
Working from home is great, but it does have drawbacks. It's hard to separate work from personal life.

TOPIC 18 加盟商機　207

Expand! （關鍵短語 1 + 1 > 2 !!）　　MP3 72

看看本單元學過的關鍵短語，還可以延伸出哪些相關說法呢？繼續擴充你的口說及寫作素材吧！

1
- **be powered by** 由⋯⋯提供能量、靠⋯⋯推動
- **be fueled by** 由⋯⋯激發催生、來自於
- **be driven by** 由⋯⋯驅使驅動、源自於

Our passion for innovation **is fueled by curiosity and determination**.
我們對創新的熱情來自於好奇心與決心。

In his acceptance speech, he said, "My success **has been fueled by** my peers, so I would like to dedicate this award to them. We did this together."
在他的得獎感言中他說，「我之所以會成功都是因為我身邊的夥伴，所以我想把這個獎獻給他們，這是我們大家共同的勝利。」

Many great innovations **are driven by a desire to solve real-world problems**.
很多劃時代的創新，背後其實就是為了解決生活中的難題。

Political decisions **are often driven by public opinion**.
政治決策往往受公眾輿論影響。

2
- **drawbacks / downsides** 有缺點或限制、不利之處
- **room for improvement** 有改進的空間

The CEO of Soulmate claimed that the new app doesn't have the typical **drawbacks** of traditional dating apps.
「靈魂伴侶」的執行長宣稱，這款新的應用程式沒有傳統交友軟體的常見缺點。

The app works fine overall, but the user interface has **room for improvement**.
這個 App 整體用起來還不錯，但使用者介面還有進步的空間。

③
- **tap into** 打入（新市場）、挖掘（資源、潛力）來取得利益與優勢
- **leverage** 有效善用……來創造最大影響力
- **draw on** 運用、借助（過去經驗、知識技能等）

The company is looking to **tap into the Asian market**.
這家公司正在努力進軍亞洲市場。

She **tapped into her creativity** to design a unique campaign.
她發揮創造力，設計了一場獨特的活動。

We need to **leverage our brand reputation** to attract more clients.
我們要善用品牌聲譽的優勢來吸引更多客戶。

The author **draws on her personal experiences** to write compelling stories.
這位作家根據自己的親身經歷來創作引人入勝的故事。

④
- **took off** 迅速成長、爆紅
- **take (something) by storm** 迅速獲得巨大的成功

His career **took off** when he got a role in a blockbuster movie.
他在參演一部大製作電影後，演藝事業一飛沖天。

The new app took the market by storm.
這個新的應用程式迅速搶佔市場，大受歡迎。

⑤
- **starting a business from scratch** 白手起家創業
- **creating something out of nothing** 從無到有創造某物
- **turning an idea into reality** 將理念付諸實踐

Your idea could change the world for the better. Never underestimate yourself. What you need to do is to figure out how to **turn your idea into reality**.
你的想法可能改變世界。別小看自己。你需要做的，只是設法將想法付諸實現。

> there are two sides to... 事情有好的一面也有壞的一面
>
> **6** It's a double-edged sword. 雙面刃、利弊參半。
>
> the other/opposite/flip side of the coin 事情的另外一面

Fame is a double-edged sword. It brings not only opportunities, but also pressure.
成名是一把雙面刃，帶來機會的同時，也帶來壓力。

Success looks glamorous, **but the other side of the coin is that** it often comes with stress and sacrifices.
成功看起來光鮮亮麗，但另一面往往是壓力與犧牲。

> **in return** 作為回報
>
> **in exchange for something** 作為交換
>
> **give and take** 互相讓步、互惠互利
>
> **7** **You scratch my back, and I'll scratch yours.** 你幫我，我幫你。
> （這種互謀其利通常會是非公開的交易、互相包庇、交換好處等）
>
> **a deal with the devil** 與魔鬼交易，指高昂的代價

A successful business partnership is all about give and take. You both have to make compromises and contributions. **In return**, you will be able to share the rewards of success.
成功的商業夥伴關係仰賴於互相讓步。你們雙方必須有所付出與妥協，這樣才能共享成功的果實。

What would you give up **in exchange for** a second chance?
你願意付出多大的代價來換得重頭來過的機會？

If an opportunity seems too good to be true, it might be **a deal with the devil**.
如果一個機會看起來好得令人難以置信，那它很可能是一個與魔鬼的交易。

TOPIC 19

Living in Space: A Future Beyond Earth
太空生活：地球之外的未來

星際殖民。

移民火星

星際旅行

Reading

MP3 73

閱讀以下文章，粗體字部分是本文的關鍵短語，先想想它們的意思及用法，再跟著引導進行更多字彙擴充練習！

There are countless books, movies, and TV shows about outer space. People have long wondered if there is life on other planets. At the same time, scientists have wondered if humans might live on the moon or elsewhere someday. Plans are now in motion to **make** this amazing possibility **a reality**.

We've already made several brief trips to the moon. As part of the USA's Apollo space program, six manned lunar landings were made between 1969 and 1972. The longest moon visits lasted about three days each. Astronauts set up temporary bases and ran experiments. On the last three visits, they used a battery-powered LRV (Lunar Rover Vehicle). The car allowed astronauts to drive many kilometers around the landing areas.

Most trips into space tend to be much closer to Earth. Since 2000, people have been living on the International Space Station, a joint project of the USA, the European Space Agency, Japan, Canada, and Russia. Astronauts staying there regularly go on "space walks" to install equipment, make repairs, and carry out scientific and medical experiments.

Now that we are so knowledgeable about living in space, where should we build colonies? Because of their closeness to Earth, the moon and Mars are the most likely locations. In fact, NASA, the USA's space agency, has a long-term plan to set up a colony on Mars. Also, China's space agency plans to send people to the moon, with a long-term goal of setting up a colony there.

However, we still face many challenges before a space colony will be possible. First, we need to **come up with** a cheaper way to transport the necessary equipment. Also, we need to find locations for colonies near a water source. **A good deal of** water will be needed for drinking, washing, and other uses. Furthermore, we need to find a way to produce fuel on the colony for cooking, heating, and trips back to Earth.

Despite these challenges, many believe **it is our destiny to** travel and live in space. Others think there are more important problems that must be addressed on Earth, such as hunger, disease, and climate change. The most optimistic people feel that improvements in technology and medicine will allow us to **meet all these challenges** at the same time. Indeed, within 50 years, a number of us may be living on another planet, looking back at Earth from a very different point of view.

翻譯

關於外太空的書籍、電影和電視節目不勝枚舉。人們長久以來一直在思考這件事情，其他行星上是否有生命存在呢？與此同時，科學家們也在思考，人類是否有一天能夠在月球或其他地方生活。現在，為了將這個令人驚嘆的可能性變為現實，許多計畫已經開始進行。

我們已經實現了幾次短暫的月球之旅。作為美國阿波羅太空計畫的一部分，1969 年到 1972 年間進行了六次載人登月。最長的登月時間約為三天。太空人建立了臨時基地並進行實驗。在最後三次登月任務中，他們使用了由電池驅動的月球車 (LRV)，這輛車使太空人能夠在登陸區域周圍行駛數公里。

大多數太空旅行通常離地球比較近。自 2000 年以來，一直有人類在國際太空站上生活，這是一個由美國、歐洲、日本、加拿大和俄羅斯共同合作的計畫。太空人定期進行「艙外活動」，安裝設備、進行修理，並進行科學和醫學實驗。

既然我們已經對在太空中生活有了這麼多了解，那麼我們應該在哪裡建立殖民地呢？由於月球和火星離地球較近，它們是最有可能的選擇。事實上，美國的太空機構 NASA 有一個長期計畫，準備在火星建立一個殖民地。此外，中國的太空機構計劃將人類送上月球，並有一個長期目標，就是在那裡建立殖民地。

然而，在太空殖民地成為現實之前，我們仍然面臨著許多挑戰。首先，我們需要找到一種更便宜的方式來運送所需的設備。此外，我們需要找到靠近水源的殖民地位置。殖民地會需要大量的水資源，用於飲用、清洗和其他用途。此外，我們須找到一種方法，在殖民地上生產燃料，用於烹飪、取暖和回到地球的旅程。

儘管面臨這些挑戰，許多人相信太空旅行和在太空中生活是人類的未來。也有些人認為地球上有更多需要解決的問題，比如飢餓、疾病和氣候變遷。而那些相當樂觀的人則認為，科技和醫學的進步將使我們能夠同時解決這些挑戰。事實上，在 50 年內，我們中的一些人可能會生活在另一顆星球上，從完全不同的角度回望地球。

Living in Space

練習 A：用英文表達 Phrase in Action

用以下關鍵短語作為句子重點提示，試著用英文表達每一句話。不一定只有一種說法！

1 make... a reality
太空旅行離我們是不是越來越近了？

> 1～3 這些短語通常用來描述目標實現、創新發想以及解決問題。

2 come up with
科學家們正試著找出在火星上種植作物的方法，這樣太空人就不需要依賴來自地球的物資。

3 meet all these challenges
如果我們能克服這些挑戰，也許就能比想像中更快在火星上生活。

4 now that
既然我們已經把人類送上月球，接下來的太空計畫會是什麼？以下是這集 Podcast 的討論重點：
太陽系之外有生命嗎？我們真的是宇宙中唯一的高等智慧生物嗎？記得追蹤我們，了解更多關於太空旅行的未來。

> 4～6 這些短語常用來鋪陳背景、引入主題，或表達信念與價值觀。

5 a good deal of
在火星建立殖民地需要大量的時間和金錢，但它可能會徹底改變人類的未來。

6 it is our destiny to
我們應該殖民其他行星嗎？有些人認為，尋找可能適合人類居住的系外行星是我們必須走上的道路，這將成為解決地球所面臨問題的方案。然而，也有人認為我們應該更加謹慎思考這件事情。撇開科學好奇心不談，我們是不是應該將重心放在拯救地球，為未來世代著想呢？

Living in Space

MP3 74

練習 B：記憶挑戰 Phrase Recall!

以下是練習 A 各句子的參考英文說法，但關鍵短語不見了！你還記得它的中文怎麼說嗎？

*Reference Only – Not the Only Way!

1（太空旅行即將成為現實）
We're getting closer to making space tourism a reality.

2（　　　　　　　　）
Scientists are trying to come up with new ways to grow food on Mars, so astronauts won't have to rely on supplies from Earth.

3（　　　　　　　　）
If we can meet all these challenges, we might be able to live on Mars sooner than we think.

4（　　　　　　　　）
Now that we've sent humans to the moon, what's next in space? Here are some highlights from this episode:
Is there life beyond our solar system? Are we alone in the universe? Follow us for more on the future of space travel.

5（　　　　　　　　　　　　）
Building a colony on Mars will take a good deal of time and money, but it could change everything for humanity.

6（　　　　　　　　　　）
Should we be colonizing other planets? Some people believe it's our destiny to find exoplanets that can support life, as a solution to the problems we are facing. However, some think we should think twice about the idea. Putting aside scientific curiosity, shouldn't we focus more on saving our planet for future generations?

Let's Chat!

練習 C：靈活應用 Phrase Remix!
同樣的短語，放進生活其他情境中應用看看！
你也可以試著造自己的句子！

1 make... a reality
高鐵的出現，讓過去不可能的生活方式變為現實：
在甲地工作、在乙地生活。

2 come up with
經過幾個小時的腦力激盪，團隊想出了一個提升使用者體驗的解決方案。

3 meet challenges
這位運動員已經訓練了許多年，準備迎接各種挑戰。

4 now that
既然大家能夠齊聚一堂，我們要盡情享受每一刻。

5 a good deal of
在幫我們的新公寓添購家電之前，我們花了超多時間在比較價格。

6 it is our destiny to
我們命中注定要相遇。

Let's Chat!

MP3 75

練習 D：記憶挑戰 Phrase Recall!

以下是練習C各句子的參考英文說法，但關鍵短語不見了，而且還變長了！試著用你的話來描述這些被標示的語言段！

Reference Only – Not the Only Way!

1 (　　　　　　　　)
The introduction of high-speed rail has made what once seemed impossible—a life of working in one city and living in another—a reality.

2 (　　　　　　　　　　　)
After hours of brainstorming, the team managed to come up with a brilliant solution to improve user experience.

3 (　　　　　　　　　)
The athlete has been training for years to meet any kind of challenge.

4 (　　　　　　　　　　)
Now that we are all here, we should make the most of it.

5 (　　　　　　　　)
We spent a good deal of time comparing prices before buying home appliances for our new apartment.

6 (　　　　　　　　　)
It's our destiny to meet each other.

TOPIC 19 太空生活   217

Expand! （關鍵短語 1 + 1 > 2 !!） 　　　MP3 76

看看本單元學過的關鍵短語，還可以延伸出哪些相關說法呢？繼續擴充你的口說及寫作素材吧！

1
　make... a reality 實現某事
　turn... into reality 將想法付諸實行
　make... happen 讓某事成真
　bring... to life 賦予生命、使其栩栩如生

You want something, go get it. **Turn big ideas into reality**.
你想要某樣東西，就去實現它。把大膽的想法變成現實。

Stay positive, work hard, **make it happen**.
保持樂觀向上，努力工作，實現目標。

The new interior design **brings the space to life**.
新的室內設計讓空間充滿活力。

2
　meet all these challenges 迎接所有這些挑戰
　rise to the occasion/challenge 成功應對困難、臨危不亂
　step up to the plate 迎難而上、挺身而出（一肩扛起責任）

Meeting all these challenges is not just our duty. It is our privilege.
應對這些挑戰不只是我們的責任，更是我們的榮幸。

No one thought he could make it, but he **rose to the occasion** and did an excellent job.
沒有人認為他能做到，但他臨危不亂，表現得非常出色。

Justine decided to face the public backlash when it became obvious no one else in the office was going to **step up to the plate**.
當團隊中沒有一個人願意負責時，Justine 決定站出來面對大眾反彈的聲浪。

3
now that 既然
given that 鑑於、既然
considering 考量到、在……情況下

Given that the world is in chaos, it's on us to make things right.
眼下局勢一團混亂，我們有責任讓一切回到正軌。

Considering what we've been through, we'll regret it forever if we quit now.
想想我們所經歷的一切，如果現在就放棄，我們永遠都會後悔。

4
a good deal of 大量的、相當多的
tons of 大量的
loads of 大量的

We don't have tons of time, but we have tons of heart. And that's enough.
我們時間有限，但我們心意無限，這就已經夠了。

Loads of people said it's impossible. And yet, here we are.
許多人都認為我們絕對不可能成功，但如今，我們做到了。

5
it is our destiny to 我們的命運／使命是
we are meant to 我們注定要
we're here to 我們在這裡是為了

It is our destiny to learn to accept what we can't change and make peace with it.
我們今生的使命就是要學會接受我們無法改變的事情，並與它和平共存。

We are meant to stand tall, even when the world tells us to kneel.
即使世界要我們屈膝，我們依然要昂首佇立。

We're here to fight for those who cannot fight for themselves.
我們的使命是為那些無法為自己而戰的人發聲。

6 **come up with** 想出、提出
figure out 弄清楚

We need to come up with something bold, and we need it fast.
我們需要想出一個大膽的計畫,而且要快。

I never thought I'd be the one **to figure this out**, but here we are.
我從沒想過會是我來解決這個問題,但是事實就是如此。

TOPIC 20

The Promise and Controversy of Stem Cells
幹細胞的潛力與爭議

幹細胞。

骨髓移植

器官複製

阿茲海默症

醫學的黃金時代

Reading

MP3 77

閱讀以下文章，粗體字部分是本文的關鍵短語，先想想它們的意思及用法，再跟著引導進行更多字彙擴充練習！

We are entering **a golden age of** medicine. Nearly every year, major breakthroughs are announced **in the fight against** disease. One of the most promising areas of research involves the use of stem cells. Although we have known about them for decades, **the flood of** discoveries in the field began in the late 1990s.

A stem cell is a cell without a specific function. It has the ability, however, to turn into any kind of specialized cell. So, for example, a stem cell could become a blood cell, a neuron, or a cell that builds muscle tissue. Stem cells can also reproduce themselves through cell division, becoming other stem cells or specialized cells.

Scientists largely focus on two kinds of stem cells. First, there are "embryonic stem cells," which divide and specialize after an embryo is formed. These cells **go on** to form our organs, muscles, bones, and so on. Because of their limitless potential, researchers feel embryonic stem cells hold the greatest hope for medical uses. As a person grows, he or she stores another kind of stem cell in the tissues, blood, and other parts of the body. These "adult stem cells" assist the body **in the event of** sickness or injury. **Depending on** where they are stored, adult stem cells turn into a specific type of cell – for the blood, bones, brain, or other organs. In July 2014, scientists used adult stem cells to grow a human cornea in a laboratory. **It was the first time** such cells were used to produce working tissue. Soon, personalized therapies using a patient's own adult stem cells may be possible.

The potential medical uses for stem cells are incredible. Since the 1960s, doctors have performed bone marrow transplants, transferring stem cells from one person to another. This treatment has been used to battle leukemia and other diseases. **The hope is that** by using adult or embryonic stem cells, doctors will be able to treat a variety of serious afflictions. Parkinson's disease and Alzheimer's disease may be among the first treated with such therapies.

Despite their promise, stem cells are not without controversy. Many people are opposed to research on embryonic stem cells if it involves killing an embryo to gather cells. There is also opposition to cloning humans or human body parts. But scientists continue to make amazing discoveries, even when working under restrictions. **They are unlocking the secrets** of stem cells one by one, bringing us ever closer to another wave of amazing medical breakthroughs.

翻譯

我們正步入醫學的黃金時代，幾乎每年都會迎來重大突破，帶來對抗疾病的新希望。其中，最具潛力的研究領域之一就是幹細胞的應用。雖然科學界早在數十年前就已經知道幹細胞的存在，但這個領域的熱潮是在 1990 年代後期才真正開始的。

幹細胞是一種尚未具備特定功能的細胞，但它具有變成各種特化細胞的能力。例如，幹細胞可以轉變為血球、神經元，或是負責建構肌肉組織的細胞。此外，幹細胞還能透過細胞分裂來自我複製，成為其他幹細胞或專門細胞。

科學家主要研究兩種類型的幹細胞。第一種是「胚胎幹細胞」，這些細胞在胚胎形成後會開始分裂並進一步發展成特定的細胞。這些細胞最終會形成人體的器官、肌肉、骨骼等。由於胚胎幹細胞具有無限的發展潛能，許多研究人員認為它們是醫學應用中最具希望的一種細胞。隨著人類成長，體內的組織、血液及其他部位會儲存另一種幹細胞，稱為「成人幹細胞」。當身體生病或受傷時，這些細胞就會發揮作用。根據儲存的位置不同，成人幹細胞可以轉變為特定類型的細胞，例如血球、骨骼細胞、腦細胞或器官細胞。2014 年 7 月，科學家成功利用成人幹細胞在實驗室中培養出人類的角膜組織，這是首次透過幹細胞製造出可運作的組織。不久後，或許能夠利用患者自身的成人幹細胞，開發出個人化療法。

幹細胞在醫療上的潛力令人驚嘆。自 1960 年代以來，醫生已經開始進行骨髓移植，透過將幹細胞從一個人移植到另一個人身上來治療疾病，例如白血病等。科學家期望未來能夠利用成人幹細胞或胚胎幹細胞，治療各種嚴重疾病，例如帕金森氏症與阿茲海默症，這兩種疾病可能會是最先受惠的案例之一。

儘管幹細胞技術前景光明，但也伴隨著不少爭議。許多人反對以摧毀胚胎的方式來取得幹細胞，還有部分人擔心人體或人體器官的複製技術所帶來的影響。然而，即使在種種限制之下，科學家仍然不斷取得驚人的發現。他們逐步解開幹細胞的奧秘，讓我們離下一波醫學革命又更近了一步。

Stem Cells

練習 A：用英文表達 Phrase in Action

用以下關鍵短語作為句子重點提示，試著用英文表達每一句話。不一定只有一種說法！

1 golden age
隨著基因療法、免疫療法和 AI 醫療診斷等等突破，我們正處於醫學的黃金時代。但我們也面臨著關於什麼是對的、什麼是公平的，還有最終什麼才是最重要的這些艱難的問題。

2 in the fight against
在對抗不治之症的這條路上，幹細胞研究帶來了新的希望。

> 1～4 的短語重在狀況描寫，常用於背景設定、文章引言。

3 a flood of
這項研究發表後，醫學中心接到了大量來自醫療記者和研究人員的電話與郵件。

4 in the event of
如果發生嚴重的太陽風暴，我們每天離不開的東西，例如手機、網銀和 GPS，可能會短暫無法使用。

5 go on
關於核融合的討論熱度仍在發酵，中國也加入了這場競賽。

6 depend on
「血月」的紅顏色深淺取決於大氣條件。

> 5～9 的短語可以用來引出背景、鋪陳因果，或強調觀點。

7 the hope is that
我們希望，透過觀察基因之間的差異，科學家能找出為什麼有些人比較容易生病。

8 it was the first time
那是科學家首次探測到低頻重力波。

9 they are unlocking the secrets
科學家正逐步揭開太陽系外行星的神秘面紗。

224

Stem Cells

MP3 78

練習 B：記憶挑戰 *Phrase Recall!*

以下是練習 A 各句子的參考英文說法，但關鍵短語不見了！你還記得它的中文怎麼說嗎？

Reference Only – Not the Only Way!

1 (　　黃金時代　　)
With breakthroughs like gene therapy, immunotherapy, and AI-driven diagnostics, we are living in a golden age of medicine. But we're also facing tough questions about what's right, what's fair, and what really matters at the end of the day.

2 (　　　　　　　　)
Stem cell research is delivering hope for new treatments in the fight against incurable diseases.

3 (　　　　　　　　)
After the new study was published, the medical center received a flood of phone calls and emails from medical journalists and researchers.

4 (　　　　　　　　)
In the event of a major solar storm, services we rely on every day such as phones, online banking, and GPS could experience temporary outages.

5 (　　　　　　　　)
The buzz around fusion energy goes on, and now China is joining the race.

6 (　　　　　　　　)
The shade of the "blood moon" depends on atmospheric conditions.

7 (　　　　　　　　)
The hope is that by looking at how our genes are different, scientists can figure out why some people get sick more easily than others.

8 (　　　　　　　　)
It was the first time scientists had detected low-frequency gravitational waves.

9 (　　　　　　　　)
Scientists are unlocking the secrets of planets beyond our solar system.

TOPIC 20 幹細胞的潛力與爭議

Let's Chat!

練習 C：靈活應用 Phrase Remix!

同樣的短語，放進生活其他情境中應用看看！
你也可以試著造自己的句子！

1 a golden age of
許多人回想童年，會覺得那是一段純真又快樂的美好歲月。

2 A flood of
大量假資訊左右了我們對這場衝突的看法，由此引發的混亂使情勢惡化，也讓更多人陷入危險。

3 in the fight against
我們總說要揭穿偽善，無論是來自社會還是內心。但會不會其實我們只是表面清高，私底下沒人看見時，早已把道德標準拋諸腦後？

4 in the event of
萬一發生大規模災難，災害應變中心在各個救災環節發揮關鍵作用，包括引導疏散、執行救援任務、搜尋失蹤人員、疏導交通以及維持公共秩序。

5 go on
「我心永恆／我心永不止息」。（電影「鐵達尼號」主題曲）

6 depend on
我本來應該要相信自己的直覺的，但我卻選擇相信你會信守承諾。

7 the first time
這是我這輩子第一次自己煮晚餐，所以準備好迎接「驚喜」吧！

8 The hope is that
希望我們一直努力爭取的一切，能為下一代創造一個更美好的世界。

9 They are unlocking the secrets
人們相信這項發現將有助於揭開宇宙的奧秘。

Let's Chat!

MP3 79

練習 D：記憶挑戰 Phrase Recall!

以下是練習 C 各句子的參考英文說法，但關鍵短語不見了，而且還變長了！試著用你的話來描述這些被標示的語言段！

*Reference Only - Not the Only Way!

1（純真又快樂的美好歲月）
Many people look back on their childhood as a golden age of innocence and pure joy.

2（　　　　　　　　　　）
A flood of misinformation shaped our views on the conflict. The resulting confusion made the situation worse and put more lives at risk.

3（　　　　　　　　　　　　）
We are constantly in the fight against hypocrisy, both in society and within ourselves. Do we claim to have high moral standards, only to break them when no one's watching?

4（　　　　　　　　　　　　　　　）
In the event of a large-scale disaster, the emergency response center plays a crucial role in various operations, including guiding evacuations, conducting rescue missions, searching for missing persons, managing traffic, and maintaining public order.

5（　　　　　　　　　　　）
"My heart will go on and on."

6（　　　　　　　　　　）
I should have trusted my gut feeling. Instead, I depended on you to keep your promise.

7（　　　　　　　　　　）
It's the first time I've cooked dinner by myself, so get ready for some "surprises"!

8（　　　　　　　　　　　）
The hope is that everything we have been fighting for will help build a better world for the next generation.

9（　　　　　　　　　　　）
The discovery is believed to hold the key to unlocking the secrets of the universe.

TOPIC 20 幹細胞的潛力與爭議　227

Expand!（關鍵短語 1 + 1 > 2 !!）　　　MP3 80

最後一個單元的 Expand！我們換個方式來學習。想像一下在不同的情境下，你會如何用中文來描述這些詞彙。這裡並沒有絕對的「標準答案」，只有相應的類似語義。試著體驗切換自如的雙語人生，這是學習中最重要的習慣——彈性。不要被僵硬呆板的「逐字對應翻譯」所限制，你日積月累的英文閱讀經驗，必定能夠滋養你在英語寫作與口語表達方面的能力。

❶ a golden age

The '90s were a golden age of music. It was a time of unparalleled variety in styles.
90 年代是音樂的黃金時代，那是一個音樂風格百花齊放的時期。

Some say the '80s were **a golden age for** action movies.
有人說 80 年代是動作片全盛時期。

Some say **the golden age of flying is never coming back**. What do you think?
有些人認為，航空的輝煌時代已經一去不復返了，你覺得呢？

The '90s **were the golden age of** Hong Kong cinema.
90 年代是香港電影最風光／輝煌的時期。

❷ in the fight against

Medical workers are **on the front lines of the fight against the pandemic**.
醫護人員站在防疫第一線守護大家。

No one can turn a blind eye to child abuse. **In the fight against it**, every effort counts.
沒有人可以對虐兒事件視而不見。防治兒少虐待，每一份心力都至關重要。

Education is key **in the fight against poverty**.
教育是翻轉貧困命運的關鍵力量。

In the fight against child trafficking, the organization has played an important role in raising public awareness.
在打擊兒童人口販賣這條道路上，這個組織讓更多人意識到問題的重要性。

3 the flood of

The flood of messages makes it hard to focus on real work.
海量的訊息會讓人很難靜下心來好好做事。
The flood of tourists during the holiday season is overwhelming for the locals.
假期期間大量湧入的遊客讓當地居民不堪負荷。

4 in the event of

In the event of an earthquake, staying calm is the most important thing.
如果發生地震的話，保持冷靜是最重要的。
In the event of a financial crisis, many businesses may not survive.
萬一遇到金融危機，許多企業可能撐不過去。
What should we do **in the event of a cyber attack**?
要是發生網路攻擊我們要怎麼辦？

5 go on

The discussion went on for more than five hours.
這場討論持續進行了五個小時。
The show must go on, no matter what happens.
不管發生什麼事情，表演還是要繼續進行下去。
What really went on at Kaohsiung Train Station that day?
那天在高雄火車站到底發生了什麼事？

6 depend on

Our decision will change **depending on the circumstances**.
我們的決定將視情況而定。
We will allocate resources **depending on the needs of each department**.
我們會根據各部門的需求來分配資源。

7 the first time

It was the first time she had ever been so honest about her feelings.
她從來沒有如此坦率地表達自己的感受過，這是第一次。
It's the first time I've done this.
這是我人生第一次做這種事情。
It's my first time visiting this place.
這是我第一次來這個地方。／我之前從來都沒有來過這裡。

8 The hope is that

The hope is that this meeting will prevent further conflict.
最理想的狀況就是透過這次會談來避免更進一步的衝突。
The hope is that our efforts will make a difference.
我們的期望是／我們希望，這些努力最終能夠帶來改變。

9 They are unlocking the secrets

Scientists **are unlocking the secrets of the human brain**.
科學家正在揭開人類大腦的神秘面紗。
Historians **are unlocking the secrets behind the letters**.
歷史學家正在解開這些信件背後的秘密。

Notes

國家圖書館出版品預行編目（CIP）資料

Phrase power! 英文短語的力量 / 劉怡均, Andrew E. Bennett 作. -- 初版. -- 臺北市：波斯納出版有限公司, 2025.07
　面；　公分

ISBN 978-626-7570-23-4（平裝）

1. CST：英語　2. CST：讀本

805.18　　　　　　　　　　　　　　　　114007986

Phrase Power 英文短語的力量

作　　者 / 劉怡均、Andrew E. Bennett（白安竹）
執行編輯 / 朱曉瑩

出　　版 / 波斯納出版有限公司
地　　址 / 100 台北市館前路 26 號 6 樓
電　　話 / (02) 2314-2525
傳　　真 / (02) 2388-0877
客服專線 / (02) 2314-3535
客服信箱 / btservice@betamedia.com.tw
郵撥帳號 / 19493777
帳戶名稱 / 波斯納出版有限公司

總 經 銷 / 時報文化出版企業股份有限公司
地　　址 / 桃園市龜山區萬壽路二段 351 號
電　　話 / (02) 2306-6842

出版日期 / 2025 年 7 月初版一刷
定　　價 / 400 元
I S B N / 978-626-7570-23-4

ⓑ 貝塔網址：www.betamedia.com.tw

本書之文字、圖形、設計均係著作權所有，若有抄襲、模仿、冒用等情事，依法追究。如有缺頁、破損、裝訂錯誤，請寄回本公司調換。

喚醒你的英文語感！

Get a Feel for English!